3013: MATED

3013: THE SERIES

Laurie Roma

The 3013 Series

3013: MATED by Laurie Roma
3013: RENEGADE by Susan Hayes
3013: CLAIMED by Laurie Roma
3013: STOWAWAY by Susan Hayes

3013: MATED

Alexis Donovan is a woman whose dream of falling in love with the perfect men has been dashed because of her infertile status. Still recovering from a war that almost destroyed the world, humans have fought to rebuild and have once again opened their shields to outside visitors. As a liaison officer for alien races that are visiting Earth, Alexis does her best to ignore what she can never have, but when she is put in charge of four visiting alien warriors, her entire world changes...

Dragons Warriors from Arcadia, Xavier and Galan Tesera and their best friends Thorn and Brydan Volis, have been curious about Earth ever since they helped the humans defeat their enemy years ago. As commanders of their own space vessel they travel the galaxies searching out the unknown, but in their hearts they know they will never truly be satisfied without a mate by their side.

When the four Dragon Warriors land on Earth they are instantly enamored with the sharp-tongued liaison who ignites a burning passion in their hearts, and know that she is the mate they have been searching for who will complete their souls. Will Alexis take a chance on four alien warriors or will the fear of leaving everything she has ever known destroy her chance of finding true love?

An Erotic Romance Novel.

3013: MATED by Laurie Roma
First Print Publication: June 2014
Print Edition

Cover design by Sloan Winters
Editing by S.L. Whitcomb

DEDICATION

To my ladies of 3013…

Thank you for sharing this world and for joining me on this journey into the future.

Prologue

The year is 3013.

Earth barely survived the Alien Wars that have ravaged the planet, and an unknown virus had nearly wiped out the entire population. On the brink of extinction, humans struggle to rebuild their civilization, although nothing would ever bring back what once was.

Enforcing martial law, a new age of mankind is born, where warriors rule and women are the ultimate prize. Only the elite earn breeding rights and are granted leave to claim a woman in pairs. Men dream of the day that they will be able to claim a woman to love, but for those chosen being claimed means the end of their freedom and a beginning to a lifelong bond with two strangers. The warriors may have the choice, but the battle for their woman's heart has only begun…

Chapter One

"You want me to what?"

Alexis Donovan stared at her commanding officer with wide eyes, not believing what she had just heard. She was one of the only top-level liaison officers in the Northwest Quadrant that was currently available, but asking her to act as the host to four visiting male warriors alone was like sending her to the badlands stripped naked and defenseless.

It was a new world in 3013.

For centuries Earth had prospered as an advanced society, coming together after the need for civil unrest had been pushed aside. Part of the healing between nations had been because of the space program. It allowed all humans to work towards a common goal, to reach for the stars and explore new possibilities. New technology such as spaceships and jump drives had changed Earth, and the advancements had enabled contact with alien races far beyond anything once imagined.

But those changes came with a price…

In the year 2960 a new alien race came to Earth called the Zyphir, and they certainly did not come in peace. The Zyphir were a colony race of insect-like creatures that stood on two feet, looking like something right out of a nightmare or horror vid. What they came for was the total annihilation of the human race, after which they would take over Earth and deplete the world of all resources until moving on to the next planet that suited their needs. A three year war ensued, during which large portions of Earth were destroyed. Not just by battle, but by an unknown virus the Zyphir carried that nearly wiped out the entire population.

Only with the help of other allied alien races was Earth finally able to defeat the Zyphir. After the war, humans struggled to survive. Martial law was declared, and the world was left under the rule of the United Federation Command Alliance, or as it was more commonly called, the Alliance.

Although the war was over, the battle had just begun to rebuild Earth to its former glory. And that wasn't so easy after the virus swept through the world, altering the genetics of the survivors. More accurately, the virus seemed to attack the female reproductive systems, leaving most women on Earth infertile. No matter how advanced medical technology had become, the cause for the infertility remained untreatable.

And so, a fertile female became the ultimate prize.

Over the last fifty years it had become mandatory for all females to be tested for fertility at the age of ten. Those that were determined fertile were tattooed with specialized scroll markings on the right side of their faces near their eye, showing the world that they were special. Those tattoos would become darker with age, turning a mercurial black when the female became of claimable age. Fertile females were also implanted with nanotechnology that made it impossible for them to get pregnant until the birth control was deactivated after their eighteenth birthdays or later when they were claimed by a pair of elite soldiers.

Infertile females were given a simple star as proof they were tested…and found lacking.

The Alliance created the harshest of punishments to ensure the safety and welfare of breedable females. The stylized markings on a fertile female's face meant that it was every soldier's duty to protect them, and all men longed for the day when they would be able to claim a woman as their own.

When a woman was chosen, the two elite soldiers that claimed her would have their initials tattooed on the left side of her face, marking her as theirs for the world to see. In return, the men would have a similar tattoo placed on their left neck, shoulder and arm as a sign of pride to have claimed a woman. These markings took the place of archaic symbols such as wedding bands to declare them a bonded unit.

At the age of ten, boys were also tested in order to determine if they would be taken for military service. Only the strongest and brightest males were chosen for the biological enhancements to become elite soldiers. The elites were bigger and stronger than normal humans, with increased reflexes and heightened senses. These enhancements were encoded into their genes, and would be passed onto their children.

Their enhanced genetics were the future of the human race.

The advantages that came with being one of the elite had caused resentment against the military that now ruled Earth, creating a new separation of classes. Although most fertile females were given genetic enhancements, some non-fertile females who pass the rigorous testing also received military enhancements to make them more productive and useful to society. As one of those females who had undergone the enhancement process, Alexis had thought that she would finally have a place where she belonged, but soon after joining the service of the Alliance, it was made clear to her that she would never be the same class as the elite male soldiers.

Alexis had worked the last six years to become a top-level liaison officer, but she knew that her male colleagues still looked down on all the female officers, her included, regardless of how well they did the job. It didn't matter though. Being an officer of the Alliance gave her life purpose. As an infertile female she would never have the dream of having two men who loved her more than life itself. She would never hold a baby in her arms or watch it grow.

Those dreams had been taken from her the moment she was tested when she was ten.

"You heard me, Officer Donovan," Director Farris barked out as he sat back in his chair behind his desk. Alexis thought his office suited his personality perfectly. It was dull, dreary and slightly uncomfortable to be in amid its stark gray on gray tones with nothing to break up the monotonous décor. The man himself wasn't any better. Reginald Farris was a tall man, with dirty blond hair worn in a standard buzz cut. Some might have called him a decent looking man, but it was his perpetual wandering eyes that made Alexis dread being around him.

"Listen, I don't have time to argue with you about this. These four visitors are last minute arrivals, and they're special. I mean VIP to the max. You know the Arcadians were essential in helping us defeat the Zyphir. If they hadn't come to our aid along with the Krytos and D'Aire we'd be bug food right now."

Damn, Alexis had to force herself not to twitch at that.

She hated bugs and just the mere mention of the Zyphir made her skin crawl, even if the Alien Wars were over before she was born. She looked at Director Reginald Farris and narrowed her eyes even as she remained standing at attention. The older man was up to something. He wouldn't have called her into his office and thrown this at her if there wasn't more to this…request.

"I understand that these are important visitors, Director Farris. What I don't understand is why I am being designated their liaison officer while they're visiting, considering there are four males." Alexis struggled to keep her voice steady, when what she really wanted to do was yell and bitch-slap the son of a bitch glaring back at her.

Since they opened their shields back up and started allowing visitors back on Earth, the Alliance had set strict guidelines on how visitations should be run. It was important that the liaison officers were well versed with the cultures that were allowed as guests on Earth's surface. Since it was standard for the liaisons to stay with visitors for the duration of their stay in a spare room at one of the spectacular guest housing locations, it was even more important that they were protected as they performed their duties.

Which was why a single female liaison officer had never been asked to host *four* males at once.

"Are you questioning my orders?" Director Farris demanded.

Well, duh...yeah. Damn right, she was.

"You will do what I tell you, Officer. The Arcadians will be—"

"Dragon Warriors, sir."

"What?"

"Arcadians who explore worlds and don't live on their home planet prefer to be called Dragon Warriors. Sir."

He waved a hand in the air, as if to brush her clarification aside. "Whatever. They will be arriving at the end of the week and you will be the officer in charge of their visit, unless..." His eyes took on a sly gleam. "I have a meeting on Delta Station in two days. I could always arrange for someone else to take on the liaison duty...if you were to accompany me on my trip."

Alexis' body went rigid and her jaw nearly drop open at the insulting insinuation. Holy hell, did the man have a few circuits loose, because clearly he had lost his damn mind. She wouldn't touch him if he were the last damn man in the entire freaking universe!

Unfortunately, this was not the first time something like this had happened to her.

She had recently been transferred from Light City here to the Capital. To outsiders it looked like a promotion, but the truth was it was nothing so simple. Alexis had actually been part of an operation that focused on identifying high ranking men that were abusing their power within the Liaison Division and removing them from office. So far, no one knew she had been part of the team working undercover, but she thought she had put all of this bullshit behind her when she transferred to the Capital.

Alexis wanted to gag as Director Farris' beady eyes glazed over with lust as his gaze roamed over her body. Even dressed in the standard uniform of a steel-gray jacket with off-center zipper, black sleeves and regulation black pants and boots, she felt dirty just from the way he was looking at her. Most people saw her pretty appearance as an asset given her chosen profession, but to Alexis, her looks were more like a curse.

Born with almost white-blonde hair and violet eyes, Alexis stood out in any crowd. When she was on duty, she usually pulled her long hair back in a ponytail, if she wasn't wearing a more formal style when she was officially on assignment with visitors. One of the perks of her position was she wasn't held to the more regimented standards of the other elite soldiers, since part of her job was looking and being approachable.

Unlike a true albino, Alexis had been blessed with the ability to tan, which made her even more unusual since she usually had light-golden skin that was striking against her other features. Adding to that, once she had gone through the genetic enhancements, her body had begun to blossom just like all the females who had undergone the change.

Where males developed more muscle mass, making them look like gods among men, women who were given the enhancements developed bodies that were more suited to sex droids. At five eight, Alexis had large breasts, a narrow waist and long legs, but she was stronger than she looked. She was trained in combat like all of the soldiers of the Alliance were, and was often underestimated.

That still didn't help her against assholes like Farris who used their positions of power to get what they wanted.

Alexis' jaw tightened, and she had to force the words out between clenched teeth when she spoke. "Sir, I will have to decline your offer and will accept the liaison position as ordered." She activated her wrist unit and waved it over the console on his desk, instantly downloading the information needed for her new assignment.

"You may want to rethink your attitude if you plan to rise in the ranks, Officer Donovan. I can be a great ally for you…or a terrible enemy if you chose to cross me."

Vile little fucker.

"I am confident in my skills as a liaison officer, sir."

Scowling at her, Director Farris narrowed his eyes. "So be it. You will do everything in your power to make sure they are well taken care of, is that understood? I don't want to hear any complaints about this assignment, no matter what happens."

"Sir."

Wanting to get the hell out of there, Alexis stood at attention and placed her right fist over her heart in salute then turned and left before he could say anything more.

Alexis let out a hiss of annoyance as she left his office and pressed a button on her wrist unit. She was glad she had gotten the entire conversation on her recorder and the fucker hadn't even noticed….the dumb ass. She took a deep breath and tried to rein in her temper as she made her way out of the Liaison Division out into the fresh air.

Putting on her sunshades, she looked out over the Capital and admired the view. She always felt a sense of pride at seeing the towering steel and glass structures that made up the city, and her mind was at ease knowing that an invisible shield protected Earth from anyone approaching uninvited.

It had once been her dream to travel the skies to other worlds far beyond what she had seen, but because of her pale eyes it was very hard due to the glaring lights that accompanied space travel. Alexis had made a few trips to nearby space stations, however she'd never be able to obtain status to be stationed anywhere but Earth because of her overly sensitive eyes.

Whatever enhancements she'd been given allowed her to see even better in the dark so she wore sunshades most of the time, except when she was talking to a higher-ranking officer. She could have asked for an assignment on one of the dark planets, but those tended to be used for prison sites and other depressing facilities that she wouldn't want to spend too much time at.

No, she was meant to stay on Earth, where she could live doing what she was good at and perhaps one day she could find a man or two to love her, despite her flaws. She watched with no small bit of envy as trios walked along the tiered walkways that connected the large buildings out in the open air. She could see the protective way the men all but surrounded the women between them, and felt an ache in her heart.

Scrolls.

That was the nickname given for the fertile women who were lucky enough to be chosen by two men. Even if she couldn't give a man a child, there was still a small chance that Alexis would find two men to join her life with, but she wasn't holding her breath.

A few years ago, Alexis thought she had been one of the lucky ones to have found an elite pair of men that could love her despite her shortcomings. She had naively believed the sweet words Draven and Cristof had given her, soaking up the attention they had bestowed upon her like a flower did the rays of the sun.

But it had all been a ruse just to get her in bed.

Both of the elite soldiers had just been biding their time until they were ready to claim a fertile woman to be their chosen. Even more insulting, now that the men had formed a bonded unit, they still offered to keep Alexis as their mistress.

And that was something she would rather die than agree to.

Once men joined the Alliance, it was common for them to quickly pair up, knowing that they would one day bond with the same woman. It was extremely rare for a single man and woman to be together, at least not in the cities where the elites reigned supreme. Even when Alexis took her first lovers, they had been a pair of men she had been in training with while still in the Academy. It had been right after they had graduated, and all three of them had known it would never go further than a brief relationship.

Draven and Cristof had been different. Their combined lust had blinded her from their true intentions every time they were together, and she hadn't realized it until it had been too late. She still remembered the day they'd broken her heart with acute clarity. They had just made love, the three of them basking in the afterglow when Draven had casually declared that they were set to claim a chosen woman the following week. Alexis' shock had been extreme. She had wanted to believe it was simply a mistake until Cristof had laughed.

"Did you really think we would bond with you, Alex? You're flawed, and we want children."

The pain Cristof's words had caused was like a stab to the heart. She had wanted to throw up when Draven had run a hand over her leg and she had scrambled out of his reach.

"We still want you, Alex. I think we always will. We just don't want to form a bonded unit with you," Draven had said, truly perplexed by her reaction.

Alexis had stumbled from their bed, fleeing as fast as her feet would carry her. It had been two weeks later when she finally saw them again. That was when they had approached her with the offer to become their mistress. Their shock at her refusal had baffled her, and so had their anger. Luckily, she had just completed her assignment and a few days later she'd transferred to the Capital.

To her surprise, a month later she learned that Draven and Cristof had also requested a transfer to the Capital. When she next saw them, both men had been furious at her for leaving without telling them. She'd told them she didn't want anything to do with them anymore, yet they'd continued to harass her. She had considered reporting them, but pride held her back. It was one thing for them to have rejected her so cruelly, but it was another to have everyone know what had happened.

It had been several months now, and although she'd done her best to avoid them, they still continued to pursue her. She had hooked up with a couple men here and there when the loneliness had become too much bear, but both times she had tried to start dating someone new, Draven and Cristof had ruined it for her. Fed up, Alexis promised herself that she would report them the next time they tried something, but she silently prayed they would simply lose interest and leave her alone.

All bonded units were not the happy relationships girls dreamed of when they were young. The fact was, most fertile females were claimed more for alliances than anything else. Basically, the system sucked for all women. Those that weren't fertile were overlooked, but those who were then became a prize to be won with little say about who claimed them.

Once a fertile female came of age, she was then declared claimable. Only females with powerful families or connections were safe from being randomly chosen by men who wanted them. And once the men had their initials tattooed on the face of their chosen, there was little anyone could do to help the woman escape her bonded unit.

Personally, Alexis thought the entire pairing system sucked, even if it was put in place to help rebuild the human race. But those who were actually chosen for love all but glowed with the radiance of happiness that they felt, and that was what Alexis wanted more than anything.

To be that happy and complete.

Pushing those depressing thoughts aside, she watched the vehicles flying in straight lines in the sky while others that chose to take ground routes drove down the streets as she used her wrist unit to make a call to Commander Jax Spartan.

Commander Spartan was one of Earth's greatest leaders and ran the Capital with an iron fist, all be it a fair one. He was a man very few people were stupid enough to challenge, and he used his authority to ensure that both members of the Alliance and citizens were protected. He was always thoughtful and deliberate in his decisions, and reported directly to the Alliance Council of Regents. The Regents were made up of retired military commanders from all of the territories, and acted as the governing body of the Alliance. The Regents looked at Commander Spartan as the epitome of what an elite soldier should be, and he took their faith in him very seriously.

Alexis trusted and respected him, but she also knew Jax on a different level. When she had gone through testing after she turned ten, her fathers had disowned her upon hearing she was infertile, claiming she was now useless. Her mother had died while giving birth to her, and her fathers had never forgiven her for that. Left in the care of the Alliance, she was sent to a one of the training facilities that catered to others like her who had been given the enhancements. Even at a young age they had to begin learning how to use their gifts.

The training was rigorous in many disciplines. Not only were they regularly tested for physical strength and endurance, they were all tested in a multitude of mental assessments that helped place them for service when they were older. The training facilities were run sort of like boarding schools, only for people like Alexis, they had nowhere to go when they were given leave.

Jax was one of the older members at the training facility, and upon arriving it had been clear to Alexis that he was a natural born leader. There was ten years separating them, but she had looked up to Jax as if he were the older brother she had never had. At that point, Jax had been a junior commander in the Academy. He had been tasked with looking out for the new recruits, and everyone at that facility followed him without hesitation.

Born an empath, the enhancements had only made Alexis' natural abilities stronger. At first she'd had a very hard time learning how to control her gift, but after a while it became second nature. More than that, Alexis had honed her gift to the point she basically became a walking lie-detector, and as a liaison officer it came in handy when she was asked to feel out the true intentions of any visitors. Jax had helped her become the officer she was today, and had always been there for her when she needed him…just like family.

"Spartan." Jax's deep voice was clipped as it sounded through the comm link, and his scowling face on the small video screen made Alexis smile.

"Commander."

"Hey, Lex," Jax's voice softened slightly with affection as soon as he saw it was her calling. "What can I do for you?"

"I need to speak to you, Commander Spartan."

The official tone of her voice had Jax's eyes narrowing at her as he barked out, "I'm in the main landing bay. Dock C. Meet me here. Now."

She chuckled as he abruptly cut off the call. She was glad she had contacted him rather than trekking all the way to the command post building where Jax's office was. Although most commanders spent their time in cushy offices, with multiple staff members running around doing their bidding, Jax was a hands-on leader. It exasperated the generals that reported to him because he was always out in the field, so to speak, since he couldn't stand being cooped up in one place for long.

Alexis opted to take one of the glides down, making her way to the main landing area in the open air instead of one of the elevators or trekking thought the underground tunnels. It wasn't far and she could use the few extra minutes to figure out what she was going to say to her commander about the incident. She knew she had to report it, but there were other things to consider. She wondered just what the hell she was going to do about her new assignment, but the most pressing issue was how she was going to stop Jax from pulverizing Director Farris into bloody dust.

Chapter Two

The main landing bay was a bevy of activity as Alexis entered the building.

Waving absently at a few officers she knew, she headed straight for Dock C. When she arrived, Alexis wasn't surprised to see Jax Spartan glaring at a few officers who looked like they had just swallowed razor blades.

Jax's stance said it all. A large, intimidating man, Jax stood at six foot eight. His thick, corded muscles bulged under his uniform as he stood with his arms crossed over his impressive chest. Feet braced apart, with a fierce frown on his face, he looked like he was seconds away from ripping the heads off the two smaller men standing in front of him.

"Commander Spartan." Alexis stood at attention and struck her fist over her heart as she waited for him to acknowledge her. She saw the entourage that followed Jax wherever he went was standing a safe distance away, out of firing range. She could feel the relief emanating from the other officers that had been getting their asses chewed who were grateful for the distraction, and she fought to hold back a smile.

Commander Jax Spartan really was an ass-kicker.

Jax slowly turned his head, focusing his intense gray eyes on her. She could see amusement flicker in his steel-gray depths before his expression hardened and he turned back to the men. "I want that report sent to me in one hour. Dismissed."

The two officers saluted then walked away as fast as they could without breaking into a run. Jax shook his head and turned to look at her with a wry grin. "I wasn't done reprimanding them, but they'll be forever grateful to you for being their savior."

"Always glad to be of service. So, what did they do to earn the wrath of Jax?" One of his brows lifted at that, making her laugh.

"Come on, Jax. Don't you know all of the Alliance calls it that when you get pissed? Actually, I think it was Archer who started it."

"Damn it," Jax growled, making Alexis laugh.

Sullivan Archer was second-in-command under Jax and his best friend. More laid back than Jax, Archer had a wicked sense of humor, but was just as capable of a commander in his own right. When they had reached elite status, they had filed together for a pairing, knowing that they would one day share a chosen woman together.

All elite soldiers had to file their partnership on record before they could claim a woman so she would know who the two men were in any bonding unit. Although it had been years since both Jax and Archer had reached elite status, both men were holding out for love before they claimed a woman.

Knowing that just made Alexis respect them more.

Despite Jax's brusque demeanor, he was a thoughtful and kind man. When they had been in the training facility together, Jax had been horrified when he discovered several of the female trainees had been abandoned by their families when they had been declared infertile. After that, he had made it a regular occurrence to take whoever was left without somewhere else to go home with him when they had leave. Jax's mother and two fathers had welcomed Alexis and the others with open arms, and for the first time she had discovered what a real family was like.

Still, she knew that any woman who took Jax and Sullivan on would need to be able to stand up to their over-the-top alpha attitudes.

Alexis sobered as she noticed the glances being cast their way. Although both Jax and Archer thought of Alexis as their sister, she had never flaunted her connection to them in front of other soldiers, or at least she tried not to. She cleared her throat. "Jax...Commander, there is something I have to report to you."

His eyes narrowed on her and she fought not to squirm. "Spit it out, Lex."

She held up her wrist unit, fighting back the embarrassment that stained her cheeks pink as she re-played the conversation she'd had with Director Farris back for Jax. She watched with increasing trepidation as Jax's jaw clenched and rage flared to life in his eyes.

"I'm going to fucking kill him," he said softly.

Uh oh.

"Umm, I don't think that—"

Jax leveled a glare at one of his minions that snapped to attention. "Barker! Get Director Reginald Farris in my office. Now!"

"Yes, sir. What should I tell him this is regarding?"

"You don't tell him shit. Just get his ass in a chair and make sure he doesn't move till I get there," Jax ordered harshly.

"Sir!"

Jax turned back to stare at Alexis as the other man ran off like the hounds of hell were at his heels. "How many other women are in your department?"

She sighed. "There are six total, well five now. Two are in bonded units who work exclusively with their men. Then there is Chloe, Morgan and I. And as you know, Skylar just got transferred out. The rest are all men."

Jax grunted. He had been the one to make Skylar's transfer happen. Where Alexis was considered a Class-A Empath, her friend Skylar Aris was a Class-A Conduit. An empath could feel the emotions of others, and had to work to keep from being swamped with those feelings so they couldn't be used in interrogation and other dangerous divisions.

Not like a conduit could.

Conduits were very rare individuals who could basically read other peoples energy, and if they were strong enough, could use that energy for their own purposes. After years of requests that had been refused by her commanding officers, Alexis had quietly brought Skylar's latest request directly to Jax. Upon seeing her credentials and ratings, he had personally granted her transfer to the interrogation unit.

"I'm not worried about Morgan. She would skin any man who came at her wrong, but you and Chloe are too nice for your own good."

Alexis jaw dropped at that. Her friends Chloe and Morgan were also infertile females, but all three of them were equally capable of taking care of themselves. Well, Morgan did have a pretty nasty temper if pushed too far.

Jax frowned at her. "You know what I mean. I'll have Director Farris replaced by tomorrow. I don't know what the hell he was thinking assigning this to you, considering it's against regulations for a single female liaison to be matched up with four male visitors."

"It's not against regulations, it's just highly unlikely that one of the directors would be stupid enough to arrange it. I think Farris was hoping I turned down the assignment and took him up on his other offer," Alexis said wryly.

"I'll take care of that son of a bitch," Jax swore then turned as another one of his aides that were forever following him called out his name. Officer Ryans panted for breath as he came to stop in front of them, his boots practically skidding on the concrete.

"Commander, sir! The Dragon Warrior visitors have arrived early and are waiting for permission to enter the shield."

Jax heaved out a sigh. "Shit, they're early. Ryans, open the shield and give them the coordinates over the Capital where they can enter our airspace. Have them land here in Dock C."

"Right away, Commander Spartan."

Officer Ryans relayed the information into his comms as he typed frantically on the tablet he held in his hand.

"Well, it looks like I'll be acting as liaison after all," Alexis said nervously. She'd thought she would have a few days to sort out the assignment, but it didn't seem like that was an option anymore. Even though she was a little worried, a part of her was excited to spend some time with visitors from Arcadia. She'd studied the Dragon Warriors, but had never actually met one in person.

Suck it up, she told herself. Shaking off her nerves, she straightened to her full height. She was a top-level officer for god's sake.

She could…would handle this assignment.

Jax crossed his arms over his chest as his eyes narrowed. "I still don't like this, Lex. I never thought Farris would be stupid enough to assign one of our female officers for this visit. You don't have to take this assignment if you're uncomfortable with it. I can order a replacement. Taking care of four men would be difficult for anyone."

"I believe she will be more than capable."

The deep voice that sounded out right behind her had Alexis spinning around, one hand on the hilt of the blaster at her hip. No one could have snuck up on both her and Jax without making a sound, not with their training.

But someone had.

Oh, my stars…

Her eyes widened at the sight of the four giant warriors that seemed to appear right out of one of her wildest, sex-starved fantasies. Standing at well over seven feet tall, far bigger than any of the elite soldiers she was used to being around, the four men towered over her with their powerfully built frames.

They each wore black leather pants paired with matching soft leather vests that left their muscular arms bare, except for the dark gold and silver tribal-looking tattoos that started on their shoulders and covered their skin down to their wrists. The marking were similar to the tattoos wore by the elite soldiers that had formed a bonding unit with a claimed woman, except the Dragon Warriors' were more far more elaborate in detail.

Obviously two sets of brothers, the first pair of warriors had long black hair that flowed loose around their broad shoulders while the other two males had dark brown hair. Each of the males had two small braids fashioned at the sides of their temples, framing strong, perfectly sculpted faces. They had powerful, chiseled jaws, high cheekbones, and lush, sensual lips that she couldn't help but wonder how they would feel pressed against hers.

Alexis' breath caught as four pairs of glowing eyes focused directly on her. The two warriors with black hair stared at her with eyes that glowed a bright silver, while the other two had iridescent golden eyes. It was like looking at the sun and moon, and those glowing eyes seemed to pierce straight into her soul.

The alien warriors ignored the elite soldiers converged in a circle around them, and continued watching her with some sort of intense scrutiny she didn't understand. It was a struggle, but Alexis tore her gaze away from them, finally able to take a deep breath now that she had broken the thrall they seemed to have over her.

She frowned as she looked around at the soldiers training their weapons on the newcomers. It wasn't often that alien visitors had the ability to transport themselves right onto the Earth's surface, but when they did it made most soldiers nervous. Officer Ryans stared at the alien warriors in awe, as did many of the other soldiers. Hell, Alexis had to admit she was still staring at them herself.

They were truly an impressive sight.

She looked back up at the giant warriors and saw what could only be described as amusement on the face of the male with golden eyes standing on the far right, while the male with silver eyes on the far left surveyed the soldiers with narrowed eyes. No matter the relaxed stances the visitors had taken, Alexis could sense that they were prepared for anything. It was in their tightly coiled muscles and their watchful gazes.

The two warriors in the middle ignored their surroundings, never once looking away from her. Both of their gazes were like a physical caress over her skin and her body heated in response. The intensity of their focus made her feel vital and alive. Christ, her reaction to them was completely inappropriate, but she couldn't help but imagine seeing their impressive bodies without clothing, sliding against hers.

Focus, Donovan.

"Perhaps we should say we come in peace," the golden-eyed brother on the right said with a sardonic smile.

Jax muttered a curse then called out to the soldiers to stand down. His voice hardened with the whip of command as he repeated the order then waited until the soldiers surrounding them warily backed away. Alexis felt rather than saw Jax standing beside her. Always the commander, Jax moved a few steps in front of her, putting himself in the position to defend her if the need arose. She watched one of the giants in the middle frown at Jax as he put a comforting hand on her arm.

"I am Xavier of the house of Tesera and this is my brother Galan," the frowning warrior with black hair and silver eyes said in a rich, deep voice. "And this is Thorn and Brydan of the house of Volis. We are Dragon Warriors from Arcadia."

All four of the giants struck a fist over their hearts in greeting.

Jax repeated the gesture. "Welcome to Earth. I'm Commander Jax Spartan. We weren't expecting you for another three or four days."

"We traveled faster than expected," Thorn said as he raised a brow in challenge. "This will not be a problem, will it?"

"No, not at all," Jax assured them. "We're very happy that you have come for a visit, and let me be the first to officially welcome you to Earth. I apologize that this is a little less formal than we usually greet our guests. We had a welcoming party arranged to meet you upon your arrival."

"We prefer this," Galan assured him. "Our visit should not cause you any trouble or any additional work."

"No trouble at all," Jax said, playing the diplomat. It always amazed Alexis how well he could slip into the role when she knew how much he hated it. Still, someone had to do it, and she was glad he was with her to greet these imposing males.

"Is this your mate?" Xavier asked, his voice a low rumble of sound.

Alexis stilled instantly. Something about the tone of his voice carried a warning of some kind…something that put her instantly on alert. Jax frowned at them and shook his head, releasing her arm as he did so as if he had forgotten that he had been touching her.

"No, this is Liaison Officer Alexis Donovan. She is the attaché scheduled to be your guide while you're on Earth, but—"

"Alexis." The way Thorn seemed to purr her name made her entire body heat up with desire. He focused those glowing golden eyes of his on her, and she felt like she was melting from the warmth she saw there. "We are honored to have one as beautiful as you to show us your world. I am sure we will be well cared for in your capable hands."

"I…ah. Thank you. The honor is all mine." Alexis cleared her throat then tried to speak again without sounding like an idiot. She looked around. "Where is your transpo?"

"We did not bring one. From the coordinates you provided we were able to transport ourselves down. We were told to arrive at Dock C, so here we are," Brydan said with a smile that showed a hint of his fangs.

Damn, even the sight of those sharp teeth was arousing.

"Right then."

Alexis had done extensive reading about the Arcadian culture. They didn't have much information on them, but what was known she had been fascinated by reading. Her heartbeat sped up as all four of them focused their glowing eyes on her again, and she struggled not to fidget under their scrutiny.

These visitors were from a far-off planet called Arcadia. She knew that long ago the males on their planet used to all be born in trios, but over the last several hundred years that had become very rare. Most males were now born as twins, while only a select grouping of couples were gifted with a male and female twin set. Others gave birth to a single female child, who was treasured greatly.

Born of magic, these Dragon Warriors were immortal shifters. Able to call forth their dragon spirit, they could shift into their dragon form at will and were pretty much indestructible. There were a very few ways that a Dragon Warrior could be killed. An example of that had been during the Alien Wars when they had come to help Earth destroy the Zyphir invaders, although no one was exactly sure how since anyone who had witnessed the event had probably died as well. The Dragon Warriors had suffered losses, but only a fraction compared to the number of human casualties that had been recorded.

Jax frowned down at her. "Are you sure about this?"

Xavier's glowing eyes flared with heat. "I hope you are not suggesting your officer is not safe with us, Commander Spartan," he growled. "We vow no harm shall come to her while she is in our care."

Alexis straightened to her full height and couldn't help but narrow her eyes at the men surrounding her. She wasn't pleased that Jax had questioned her in front of the visitors, nor did she like the way Xavier seemed to think they would be taking care of her when it was supposed to be the other way around. "As the Liaison Officer in charge while you're visiting our planet, I promise you'll be safe while in *my* care."

All four males smiled at her words, giving her a jittery feeling in her belly. She saw amusement flash in their glowing eyes and was confused by the warmth she felt pouring from them that seemed to be directed toward her.

Christ, they were really, really sexy for aliens…with fangs.

"Excellent," Brydan said, practically purring the word. "We would like for you to show us our living quarters now."

"Yes, of course," Alexis said, remembering her place as their guide. She checked her wrist unit and saw that Jax's aide had already forwarded her the itinerary for the Dragon Warriors' stay, and the location of where they were to be staying. She looked over at Officer Ryans with a grateful smile which he returned with a slight blush.

Feeling waves of anger coming from the visitors, Alexis turned to look up at the giants to find all four of them frowning at her. Thinking they were impatient to get to their quarters, she hurried to explain, "Officer Ryans just sent me the location where you will be staying. I can escort you there now."

She was relieved when they smiled at her again and the emotions pouring off of them seemed to calm. They were more difficult to read than humans, but for a moment their anger had been palpable, just as it had been when Jax had first introduced her. It confused her and threw her off balance, but she couldn't worry about that now. She had a job to do.

Turning to Jax, she saluted him. "Commander."

He returned the gesture then ordered, "You are to report in to me at the end of the day. Is that clear, Officer Donovan?"

"Yes, sir." She barely held back the urge to roll her eyes at him, but she could tell he knew what she was thinking when his lip curled in a slight smirk. She knew he just wanted to check in with her later to make sure she was okay, and she couldn't be irritated at him for being a good friend. Turning back to the four male warriors she would be spending the next few weeks with, she made sure she had her game face on. "If you would please follow me…"

"Wherever you lead, my lady," Thorn said low enough that she wasn't sure if she heard him correctly.

Heading out of the landing bay, Alexis was acutely aware of the four large males that seemed to surround her like her own personal wall of protection as she led them out into the fresh, open air. The day was nearly perfect, with brilliant blue skies and puffy white clouds. She put on her sunshades and noted how all four males frowned at her as she did.

"You will be staying at one of the suites in that building there," she said, pointing to a tall tower of glass and steel across the large courtyard from them as they exited the building where the landing bays were located. As they walked, she noticed many of the citizens and soldiers gawking at the Dragon Warriors by her side. "I apologize in advance if people stare at you. You are bigger than the men on our planet—"

"We can see that. Have no fear, Lexie. You have nothing to apologize for. We are big…and we know it," Brydan said with a wink.

She couldn't help when her body flushed under his attention and she had to force her gaze not to stray below his belt. Yeah, she bet they were big all over. Clearing her throat, she focused on walking without tripping on something. The four of them were putting off some potent sexual vibes and it was clouding her head with lust.

"Things have changed greatly since we were last here," Galan murmured softly as he looked around. "I forgot how pleasing your blue sky is to look at."

Alexis looked over at him in surprise. "You've been to Earth before?"

"Aye. During what you call the alien wars."

She slowed down and came to a stop as she gaped at him. "But that was…"

Brydan smiled down at her, his gold eyes glowing with amusement. "We are almost two hundred years old, beauty. We fought in your war against the Zyphir and lost many friends in the years it took to defeat the invaders."

"Oh, wow," she whispered reverently. Impressed beyond belief, she couldn't believe she was the liaison for real life heroes…living legends. These males were warriors who had come to Earth's aid, and they had never asked for anything in return. It was a privilege to host them and she wouldn't do anything to screw up this assignment. "On behalf of our planet, I would like to thank you for everything you did for us."

"No need. Truly. We always appreciate a good battle," Brydan said jovially. "And we were pleased to be of service…especially if it meant you survived."

That was a strange way of putting it, and Alexis couldn't help but think there was more to what he had said.

"Those were dark days," Thorn commented as he looked around. "But your people have come back from the ashes of the destruction and have risen again."

"We have," Alexis agreed proudly as she started to walk again. She noticed that all four males kept their attention on her, even as they noted everything around them, including the number of people that watched them pass. "I've read about your race. Well, as much as I could, I guess. There isn't a lot on file about you. I know you like to be called Dragon Warriors since you are travelers instead of Arcadians, right?"

"Aye, it is easier to be known throughout the universe as such," Galan explained, making Alexis smile. "It allows other cultures to know what we are, which can stop them from starting unnecessary trouble with us and cuts down on explanations."

"It also shows the distinction of who we are to our own people," Xavier added. "Arcadians are those who live on our home world of Arcadia. As Dragon Warriors, although we may visit, our home is amongst the stars aboard our vessel, *the Odyssey*."

"You must love it, traveling to other worlds," Alexis said wistfully.

"We do, but it can be lonely. You have a desire to travel?" Thorn asked, his voice serious.

"I do, but I can't. My eyes are very sensitive and the harsh lighting on most space vessels hurts me."

"But if the light did not hurt you, would you want to travel?" Thorn insisted with an intensity she didn't understand.

Alexis thought fleetingly about her dream to travel the stars and smiled. "Yes, I suppose I would."

She led them onto the glide that took them up to the entrance of their temporary residence. "We use an implant similar to your own technology that converts languages so most citizens in the cities will be able to understand you. But if you run into anyone who doesn't, please just let me know and I can translate for you."

At their nod, she turned to face forward on the glide. Grateful for the momentary respite from their intense gazes, she froze in place as she felt a gentle touch as if one of the men behind her had run his hand over her ponytail. The weight was gone before she could turn and she figured she must have imagined it.

Closing her eyes, she tried to regain control of her body when all she wanted to do was turn around and throw herself in the arms of one of them. Hell, it didn't matter which one. She was extremely attracted to all four, and that unnerved her. They were pure temptation with their gorgeous, big bodies and handsome faces. It was going to kill her not to give into the lust raging through her body, but she had to keep herself in check.

Since meeting the four alien warriors she had become one big mass of hormones. Never had she been so instantly attracted to anyone, let alone four men at once. They were forbidden, totally off limits. She had a personal rule not to get involved with anyone she was working with, plus it would go against every professional standard of her rank, as well as causing potential intergalactic implications if she gave into her urges.

She knew she should probably hand this assignment over to someone else, and had been fully prepared to do so…until she saw them. After she saw them she knew she wouldn't be handing the assignment over to anyone else. Something about the strong warriors drew her, making her want to spend more time with them, even if it was torture for her self-control.

No, these males were not for her, but damned if she couldn't appreciate the eye candy.

Stepping off the glide, she used the code that had been given to her to gain entry into the building. She led them onto the lift and pressed in another series of numbers on the panel that would take them directly to the suite that had been prepared for their use.

Being surrounded by the four massive bodies in the elevator made it impossible for Alexis to ignore their potent appeal. Thankfully, it only took a matter of seconds to rise up the floors, and when the doors opened she walked out into the spacious suite that was well suited for such large males.

This particular suite had been enlarged with higher ceilings than usual and sturdier furnishings to suit visitors like the Dragon Warriors. The suite ran the entire floor of the building and had eight full bedrooms and a large central gathering area with a full kitchen off to the side. This particular suite also had a large garden out on the balcony as well as a small pool for them to enjoy.

She took off her sunshades and surveyed the room, pleased that everything was in order. She always loved staying at one of the visitor suites since they were so much nicer than her own living quarters. Still, some of the visitors she had hosted had made it almost impossible to enjoy her time in the suites, but she had a feeling these four wouldn't give her that kind of problem.

Christ, with the way she was feeling, she was more likely to lock the doors…with them inside the suite with her. Mentally scolding herself again, she reminded herself to do her job. "Well, here are your temporary living quarters. I hope it's—"

Her words were cut off as she turned to find Xavier standing right behind her, his glowing silver eyes piercing into her as she tilted her head back. She was frozen in place as he slowly reached out and took the sunshades from her shaking hand.

"You fear me?"

"I…no, I don't. It's just that I didn't expect you to be standing behind me." Yeah, fear was definitely not what she was feeling with him so close to her.

He seemed to study her and her eyes widened as he reached up and gently pushed a strand of her hair off of her face that had come loose from her ponytail. "I do not like these," he said holding up her sunshades.

Confusion had her brow furrowing. "You don't?"

"Nay, they hide your beautiful eyes from our view, but I understand they protect you so I will not destroy them."

She frowned at that. Taking them back, she slipped her sunshades into her pocket to protect them in case he changed his mind. No fucking way was she going to let him destroy her sunshades. She was ready to blast him with censure, but was distracted when he smiled down at her, flashing his fangs as he did.

"I am curious about something…" Xavier said, stepping even closer so she had to tilt her head back to maintain eye contact with him.

She tried to calm her rapidly beating heart as she fought the urge to step back. His closeness didn't frighten her, but she was afraid she might jump him if he got any closer. Her hands trembled with the desire to touch him. His scent was intoxicating and his powerful body made her want to rub herself against him. Shaking off the feeling, she tried to smile at him. "Please, feel free to ask whatever you want. I will answer whatever I can for you while you are visiting. That's why I'm here."

The others moved as one so they were effectively blocking her in, making her eyes widen and her pulse speed up. Excitement mixed with apprehension as she felt Thorn at her back while the others stood at her sides. She'd never felt so small and feminine before, and became all too aware that she was alone with four of the largest males she had ever seen.

Her heart thudded in her chest and her knees grew weak as their emotions swamped her with lust too powerful to ignore. She felt her pussy weep in response, spilling the proof her of desire for them as an embarrassed blush heated her cheeks.

Suddenly, taking this assignment didn't seem like a very good idea.

Alexis watched as they inhaled deep, drawing in her scent and she knew they smelled her arousal. She'd read enough about them to know about their enhanced sense of smell and her embarrassment changed to pure mortification.

Yep, she was fucked…and not in a good way.

"Calm, little one," Xavier murmured as he lifted a large hand and gently stroked over the star tattoo next to her right eye. "What is this mark you wear? We have noticed females with this and others who wear a different symbol."

Nothing he could have asked could have killed the lust she was feeling quicker than the reminder of her personal shame. Her jaw clenched against the pain as she struggled to calm the emotions swirling around inside her. "It is the symbol that marks me a flawed woman," she explained, her voice void of all emotion.

Holy shit!

She wasn't expecting the reaction she got when all four of them growled furiously. The low, vicious sound was frightening and made her freeze faster than if someone was holding a blaster to her throat, but with them surrounding her she had nowhere to go.

Xavier used his hand to tilt her chin up, and she found herself staring into silver eyes glowing bright with fury.

"Who dared to call you flawed?"

Chapter Three

Xavier barely held back a snarl of rage as he looked down at the tiny human female staring up at him with wide eyes the prettiest shade of violet he had ever seen in all the worlds he had ever visited.

But she wasn't just any female…she was his mate.

As a dragon shifter and keeper of magic, Xavier was a male with immense power, far beyond anything humans could ever imagine. With his brother Galan and his two best friends and blood brothers, Thorn and Brydan, there was very little they could not accomplish. No task was too great or out of their reach, and what he wanted most right at the moment was to go out and find every single living creature that had dared insult his little female and destroy them.

Alexis belonged to them…even if she didn't know it yet, and no one would ever harm her ever again. She was their mate, or she would be once they claimed her, and it was their duty and privilege to care for her.

From the moment they had arrived on Earth, Xavier had been overwhelmed with the need to claim Alexis. All it had taken was one look, one smell of her scent and he knew without a doubt she was the one they had been looking for their entire lives. He had felt something settle inside his soul, as if he had finally found the missing piece of himself that allowed him to really breathe for the first time, and knew it was the same for Galan, Thorn and Brydan.

Dragon Warriors wished to find their mate more than anything. They were immortal, and the long years became harder to bear without the one female they would love above all else. Most males were born in twin sets, and all had dark, golden skin with dark hair and features. For those males that chose to live their lives away from their home world of Arcadia, it was a lonely existence.

Despite the hardships, the need to explore was ingrained into their very being.

Years ago, when Xavier and Galan had realized they wanted to leave home, it was only fitting to ask their closest friends, Thorn and Brydan, to join them. Their parents had been the best of friends and it was natural that the four males had formed a close friendship growing up. Since they were younglings, Xavier had always been the leader of their group. Strong and commanding, he took charge of every situation. His twin Galan was the complete opposite of him. Quiet and reserved, some thought him shy, but the truth was that he was a dreamer with a poet's soul. Thorn was a planner and saw everything, while his brother Brydan was a trouble maker with a wicked sense of wit.

The four of them were very different, but together they created an unstoppable force. They had always acknowledged that their close bond would make it necessary to take a single mate to share among them. They loved traveling the stars, but their desire for a mate who would love them had grown into a hunger that was too strong to ignore.

The four of them had received plenty of offers from females on numerous worlds they had visited. Most females seemed to be drawn to their strong bodies and dark looks. Sometimes they would sate their lust, but never before had all four of them looked at one female and knew she belonged to them.

Not until they saw Alexis Donovan.

She was a vision more beautiful than he could have ever imagined in his wildest fantasies. The tiny female had pale hair the color of a sunbeam, and shocking eyes that reminded him of the purple moons from their homeland. He knew instantly that she would be the one to complete his soul, and the urge to claim her rode him hard. Xavier's body had grown tight and his cock had hardened the moment their eyes had met. He had also felt the surge of lust from his brother and friends and knew they were in complete accord.

"She is the one," Galan had declared through their mind link the moment they had transported to the Earth's surface.

"Aye, she is," Xavier had responded, feeling a wealth of satisfaction surge through him.

"Let us claim her now and be done with this," Brydan had growled impatiently. *"We could be gone and bedding her before the humans know what happened."*

"Tread carefully, brother," Thorn had warned. *"She is a human representative and we do not want to start a war with Earth if we claim her."*

That had Xavier going still, and had sent anger surging through him. *"If? There is no if, Thorn. She is our mate. Can you not feel it?"*

"Aye, I do, but what if she is taken or does not want us?" Thorn shot back. *"And how willing would she be to mate with us if we cause a war with her people?"*

Damn Thorn and his logic.

But hearing that her people deemed her unworthy changed things.

"Calm, brother," Galan said, using their blood bond to speak telepathically instead of out loud as Xavier fought the urge to shift.

Never before had he felt such rage coursing through his veins. How dare they call her flawed? She was perfection, every inch of her lush body, and anyone who said different would learn that they would have to answer to him.

"To all of us," Brydan corrected.

"Calm, both of you," Thorn warned softly. *"You are scaring her."*

Xavier took a deep breath, trying to regain control over his emotions. The last thing he wanted to do was frighten his mate before he had a chance to bond with her. But looking at her he didn't see fear, he saw astonishment instead.

"You…you're very angry," she whispered, her voice filled with surprise.

"Aye, I am, but not at you. You are not frightened of me because you know I would never harm you," Xavier stated. It wasn't a question. No, he was too arrogant for that.

Her lips curved up in a small smile that made his heart race. "No. I'm just surprised that you are angry on my behalf."

Insult had his eyes narrowing on her. From the sound of the growls coming from Galan, Thorn and Brydan, they obviously felt the same way.

Her head jerked to the side, looking at the other males then settled back on Xavier's face. He watched as she gulped, and couldn't help but imagine her doing that while drinking down his seed. He held back a groan as he shifted his stance to ease the pain of his erection trapped inside his leather pants. If he didn't get her under him soon he felt like he was going to die.

"Why is this such a surprise to you?"

She sputtered for a moment, not knowing what to say then she simply shrugged. Xavier was not satisfied with that response and would have questioned her further if her wrist unit didn't beep.

He stepped back, allowing her to leave the cocoon they had created around her and immediately felt bereft at the loss of her nearness. They watched her silently as she moved across the room and answered the call. No matter how far she had moved from them, they were still able to hear the call with their enhanced hearing and relaxed as they realized she was speaking to her commander.

"I need her," Xavier whispered, all the longing and need he felt clear in his tone.

"We all do, but I fear rushing her into a mating that she does not understand," Thorn replied.

Brydan blew out an impatient breath. *"I still say we should just take her with us and leave. Once she is truly ours we can return to visit."*

"I wonder how you ever have female company," Galan growled in disgust, making Brydan grin.

"I have never had one complain yet, my friend."

Brydan's low laughter had Alexis turning back toward them, smiling at the sound. The four males straightened as she walked back to join them, her eyes filled with hesitation. "That was my commander. There has been an informal dinner planned for this evening if you're willing to attend. We have a larger celebration planned at the end of the week but—"

"Would you like to go to this dinner?" Brydan asked.

She frowned. "That's not up to me. This is your—"

Galan stepped closer and cupped the side of her face in his large hand, rubbing his thumb over her cheek as if savoring the feel of her. "We have no preference except to spend more time with you. If you would like to attend then we shall."

"I…okay. Yes, I'd like to go."

Galan nodded. "Then we will be happy to go wherever you wish."

She cleared her throat and took a step back, looking around at the four of them. "I'm sorry, I wasn't prepared for your arrival yet. I have to go back to my living quarters to pick up a few things. As a liaison officer, we usually stay with the visitors we are in charge of looking after. That is, if it's alright with you if I stay here…in case you need anything."

"We would love for you to stay with us," Thorn said so reverently that it had her blinking.

Thorn glanced at Xavier, reading the sharp hunger flooding through their link. He knew Xavier was close to losing his mind with the need for her, not that he wasn't. But Thorn knew that Xavier had always been closer to the dragon spirit that lived within them, and it was more difficult for his friend to control his animal nature. *"You and Galan go with her. Prepare her for what is to come, and by the goddess, explain to her what it is we want before pouncing on her."*

Xavier looked at Thorn with gratitude glowing bright in his molten silver eyes. *"Thank you, my friend. I will do my best to convince her to bond with us."*

"Just try not scare her."

"All will be well," Galan promised. *"We will allow no other outcome. She belongs to us. All four of us."*

"This bites," Brydan grumbled. *"Since Thorn and I will have to wait for our turn to bond with her, at least keep our mind link open so we can experience her pleasure that way."*

Xavier and Galan nodded then smiled as Alexis shot them a confused look. "We shall accompany you to your domicile to collect your things," Xavier said.

"Oh, well…"

"Thorn and Brydan will stay here to relax for a bit while my brother and I join you," Galan said, making Brydan snort. "It will be interesting to see where you reside."

Before she could argue, Xavier took her small hand in his. "We do not wish to be parted with you, and would feel better if we could come with you to offer our protection."

Her brows shot up at that then she sighed. "I'll be fine, but you can come with me if you really want."

"We do."

The looks of satisfaction on their faces gave her pause, but figured she could take them with her if they really wanted to go with her. Really, they were just curious.

What could happen if she took them home with her?

Alexis fidgeted uncomfortably as she led Xavier and Galan to her living quarters.

Acutely aware of the curious eyes on them as they walked down the street together, she led them toward the building she lived in that catered to elites. The large men stubbornly refused to leave her sides, which meant other people had to move out of their way. Of course, most people would have moved anyway, considering how big the Dragon Warriors were.

They were like her own personal force field.

Their glowing eyes seemed to scan the street as if searching for some unseen threat. Their big bodies shielded her protectively, as if she were the most important person in the world to them. It was an amazing feeling, yet also slightly bewildering.

And it made her heart ache with longing.

They were large men and very intimidating…not to mention so wickedly handsome she felt the need to change her clothes when she got home because she was sure her panties were soaking wet. She wanted to cringe as the men at her sides took a deep breath, closing their eyes as if to savor the scent. They had been doing that ever since they had left the guest suite. She hoped to god that they were scenting the savory smells of food drifting from the various restaurants they'd walked past instead of her lust for them.

The scene back at the visitors suite had her confused, and being around Xavier and Galan wasn't allowing her to process what had happened in peace. All four of the men had been killing her with the waves of lust pouring off of them. When they had closed her in between their massive bodies she had been close to ripping off their clothing and begging them to take her.

Never before had she felt so connected to anyone, and it baffled her even more because the intense desire hadn't been for one or two of them.

She wanted all four of them.

Needing to get the hell out of that room before she did something she'd regret, she had taken the opportunity Jax's phone call had afforded her and said she had to leave. She'd never expected them to want to join her.

"Hey, Lexie!"

Alexis turned as she heard the sound of her friend Skylar's voice calling her. She smiled as the other woman hurried over.

"Hi, Skylar," Alexis greeted the other woman warmly. She introduced Xavier and Galan to her friend, covertly watching them for their reaction. Skylar Aris was a beautiful woman, tall with the perfect body of an enhanced elite, and long black hair she usually had pulled back in a bun, but was now falling over her shoulders in sexy waves.

All men reacted to Skylar's beauty, much to her friend's consternation. She usually had the ability to make men speechless with one look of her eerily light-blue eyes, but Xavier and Galan seemed…unaffected. Puzzlement rocked Alexis back a mental step. She had been so certain the males would forget about her as soon as they met another beautiful woman, but the only thing she sensed from them was mild curiosity.

"It is nice to meet a friend of Alexis," Xavier said in his deep, rich voice as he casually placed a hand around Alexis' waist, pulling her to him. Galan stepped closer so he was practically pressed to her other side. Skylar's eyes widened as she watched them and Alexis was even more bewildered by their possessive display.

"Ah, nice to meet you as well."

"Are you ready to move?" Alexis said, trying to act normal when she was feeling anything but. Her heart was racing at the feel of Xavier and Galan's heated skin against hers even through their layers of clothing. She had to stop from simply closing her eyes and enjoying the feeling of Xavier's hand rubbing her side gently as they stood there and forced herself to focus on the conversation.

"Almost. I have a month before I actually start with the new unit they're putting together. I sure will miss you. Who knows where they will station us."

Alexis laughed, glad for the distraction. "You'll be too busy with your new unit to miss me." She turned to look up at the men at her side. "Skylar used to be a liaison officer, but she just transferred to the interrogation unit."

"What is that?" Galan asked.

Skylar smiled. "We investigate crimes. It's going to be so exciting. I can't wait to start, but I can't help wishing you were coming with me."

Xavier frowned. "This interrogation unit sounds dangerous. I would not want Alexis doing anything that could put her in peril."

"And you think being a liaison for alien races never puts liaison officers in danger?" Skylar laughed. "Lexie, you should tell them some of the more exciting stories…especially the one about the Reema group last month. Boy, were they a pushy bunch."

Alexis flushed at the memory then paled as she felt a flood of rage coming from the men so strong it almost brought her to her knees. The sensation was so much stronger since she was touching them that she hadn't been prepared for the rush of feelings. Gasping, she found herself in Galan's strong arms, the front of their bodies plastered together as he held her up.

"What is it, sweetling? Are you unwell?"

"No, I'm fine," she lied. Her senses were calmed by the concern she felt from him, but the steel-hard spike of his erection pressing against her had her freaking out for a completely different reason. Reminding herself they were on a street where anyone could be watching her unprofessional behavior, she took a deep breath and fought the urge to hump his leg to gain some relief.

"Please put me down."

Galan's jaw clenched, but he did as she asked, holding onto her as her feet touched the ground. "I believe I should carry you to your domicile."

"I'm fine, really." Alexis found herself rubbing her hands on his arms. She told herself it was to soothe him and not just because she wanted to touch him. Feeling the waves of pleasure coming from him, she smiled shyly before stepping back only to bump into Xavier. He stroked a hand over her hair and the gentle touch made her want to purr with pleasure.

Holy jump drives, what was wrong with her?

"Ah, Alexis? Could I have a minute?"

"Sure," Alexis said, blushing at her behavior. With her head down she excused herself from the two Dragon Warriors then walked a few feet away with her friend.

"What the hell is going on? First of all, those are two of the hottest men I have ever seen, and honey, they are all over you," Skylar said in a rush. "Go, Lex!"

"I don't know what is happening to me," Alexis groaned. "Ever since I met them I've been unable to control myself. And it's not just these two. There are two more back at the suite."

"Four? Seriously? You lucky bitch," Skylar hissed as she grinned.

"Sky, I can't. You know I would get fired if I let anything happen. And I don't think I can be around them anymore without something happening. I can't seem to control myself around them."

Sympathy clouded Skylar's eyes then they took on a speculative gleam. "Why the hell should you control yourself? No one has to know. And it's not like you'd be the first officer to indulge a little. Plus, you deserve some happiness after what those assholes put you through. Don't hold back just because of the job."

"You think? I mean, I feel that they want me, but I don't know if it's me or they just want to be with a human woman."

"I don't think that's it. They barely looked at me when I joined you, and I'm sensing some crazy shit coming from you guys. When I came over, their energy was surrounding you, and yours was merging with theirs. It still is. It's like their energy is reaching for you even though we are standing over here. And honey, they are watching you like they want to eat you alive. I say, let them."

Alexis shivered at the image that generated in her head. She wanted them with a passion she'd never felt before, and it seemed they wanted her as well. Could she really have a fling with them knowing that it could cost her everything when she had never done anything like this before? Looking over at them to find their glowing eyes were locked on her, she decided it was worth it.

For one night with them she would risk it all.

"Jesus, you three need somewhere private before you combust. Your energy flare-ups are starting to affect me. I love you and all, but this is just pervy."

Alexis didn't even look over as she heard Skylar's statement. "See you later, Sky."

Skylar chuckled. "Yeah, I'll see you."

Alexis walked back over to Xavier and Galan with her eyes on theirs. She looked down as they both held out a large hand to her.

"Take us home with you, Alexis."

Taking a deep breath, she placed her hands in theirs and did exactly that.

When they reached her living quarters she was surprised, and slightly disappointed that one of them didn't just pick her up and slam her back against the closed door. Instead, both men glanced around her one bedroom unit, looking very out of place in the small room.

She had a nice place, but it was nowhere near as opulent as the guest suites were. Feeling awkward, she pushed away from where she had been leaning against the wall watching them. "If you will just give me a few minutes I can pack a bag and—"

Her words were cut off as she was whirled around. She slammed against Xavier's hard body as he hauled her up against him. "You know that we want you."

"Yes," she admitted breathlessly.

His eyes narrowed. "But you doubt our sincerity? There will be no untruths between us. Ever."

Speechless, she looked at him with wide eyes. Shit, had they hear her conversation with Skylar? She felt herself pulled gently out of Xavier's hold as she was lifted into Galan's arms.

"This is how I wanted to hold you earlier, but I did not want to embarrass you in front of your people."

She wrapped her arms around his neck as he carried her over to her couch. Sitting down, he positioned her on his lap and she felt his hard cock nestled under her ass. She curled into him as Xavier stomped over to stand in front of them, his silver glowing eyes bright with anger.

"Why are you so mad?" she whispered.

"Do you really think we want you just because you are the first human we encountered?"

Alexis gaped at him. Shit! They *had* heard her talking to Skylar!

She floundered for something to say then decided to just go with the truth since they seemed to be able to read her almost as well as she did them. "I'm an empath." She saw their eyes widen in shock and hurried to continue. "I can't always sense what you are feeling, but when your emotions are strong or when you're touching me, it's easier."

"Then you can sense how much we need you," Galan said cautiously.

"I can feel your lust. Yes," she clarified.

"What we want from you goes far beyond lust, little one," Xavier said, his glowing eyes burning bright with some unrecognizable emotion. To her surprise he pushed the coffee table out of the way and went to his knees in front of where she was perched on Galan's lap. "We want more than one night with you. What we ask is far more than you might be willing to give, but we will do our very best to make you happy if you choose to give yourself to us."

Alexis stiffened, unsure what he was saying. "I…I don't know what you mean."

Galan used his hand to move her chin so she was staring up at him. "We want to claim you as our mate, Alexis."

Shock had her reeling. They couldn't be serious. That was like…permanent! They had just met a few hours ago, how the hell could they want a lifelong commitment with her? She licked her dry lips nervously and heard both men groan. Ignoring the waves of lust pouring from them she struggled to understand what they were saying.

"How can you say that? You don't even know me!"

Xavier reached out and placed a large hand on her chest, right over her frantically beating heart. The heat of his skin was like a soothing balm, and her body hummed with anticipation. There was sheer determination shining back at her as she met his gaze.

"Since the first moment we saw you, we felt the mating pull. We have searched worlds for the one who would complete us, and we know it is you. You are the one we have been waiting for."

"But it would not just be us. It would be Thorn and Brydan as well," Galan added. "As Dragon Warriors, we travel the universe searching for other life and knowledge we can send back to share with our people. But all Dragon Warriors travel with companions. Usually another twinset or two, so the long journey is not as hard to bear."

"As brothers, Galan and I share a bond from birth that means we share all thoughts and memories of the previous day each rising, like a mind merge. But we also have a blood bond with Thorn and Brydan that means we all must take the same mate."

Alexis frowned as she struggled to keep up with what they were telling her, not entirely sure she liked the idea, but she was also intrigued. “So, you want to share me with your friends?”

Galan shook his head. “It is not like you mean. You must understand that over the last hundred years we have formed a blood bond with Thorn and Brydan that is almost as strong as the one I have with my brother. It has aided us in battle, allowing us to read one another as if we are one. This means that when we touch you, they will know it and crave you just as deeply as we do.”

“We have known for a long time that all four of us would claim the same female, but you need to be prepared to have four mates instead of two,” Xavier explained. “We want you to understand that we need you to accept all of us into your life…and into your heart. If you do, we will make sure you never regret leaving with us.”

“Wait!” she cried out as Xavier reached for her and she saw the hurt cloud his glowing eyes. She wanted to soothe him, but she was dizzy with what she just learned and couldn’t focus on anything else. Holy hell, she needed to think! Getting up, she felt Galan’s hesitation as he released her so she could pace the room.

“Leave with you? So, the four of you want to mate with me, but what does that mean? You want me to travel with you? I’m so confused.” Talk about shocking the shit out of a girl! This was definitely not what she expected when she woke up this morning.

Xavier couldn’t take it any longer. He stormed over to her and grabbed her by the arms, holding her in place. “We want you for our mate,” he growled. “You feel it. You were meant for us.”

“But I don’t know what that means!” Alexis cried out. “All the information that I have on your people doesn’t say anything about what mating actually is!”

“Then let us show you,” Xavier said a second before he slammed his mouth down onto hers.

Chapter Four

Oh, stars...

Alexis' breath caught as she was swamped with the greatest pleasure she'd ever encountered before, her senses bombarded with a combination of his lust and her own. Xavier's kiss was intoxicating as they fed off one another and she wanted more...needed more. Their tongues tangled together, stroking, tasting and she gasped as his sharp fangs nicked her lip.

She was panting as she was spun around and pulled forcefully into Galan's arms. Caught off balance, she fell against his hard body. Her mind slow to comprehend what was going on when all she wanted was Xavier's lips back on hers, to feel both of them touching her.

"Do not bond her!" Galan growled harshly.

Xavier let out a vicious snarl like a wounded animal as he stomped away from them. Alexis' eyes widened as she watched him. Now that the pleasure had abated slightly so she was able to think, the ache in her lip became more noticeable. She reached up and touched her lower lip and pulled her fingers back to find a small trace of blood on them.

Galan gently cupped her face so she was facing him, his glowing eyes bright with hunger. "We do not want to force you into mating us before you are ready, but it is difficult for us to hold back our nature. If you mate with us we will need to create a blood bond with you."

Well, shit...

"You mean you have to drink my blood? Like a vampire?"

"Just a little, and nay, it is not like a vampire. It is more of an exchange. If we drink from you it will allow us to feel what you do and make it so we can communicate in our minds. We can wait for you to decide to complete the ritual that will make you ours, but if you do we will need this to feel closer to you."

"Damn it! You give her the means to escape us!" Xavier snarled through their bond.

"I am giving us the means to have her, you bloody fool!" Galan snapped back. *"I will not force the blood bond on her, and she cannot take our blood without beginning the conversion. If we do that before she is ready, we will lose her trust. You heard her friend. Others have betrayed her in the past. I will not begin our mating that way."*

Xavier let out a breath, calming himself. *"You are right, brother. But this pains me not to bind her to us."*

"For me as well, but we cannot break her trust. Control, brother."

Xavier growled low in his throat at the reprimand. The need to feel Alexis in his arms, to claim her, was bordering on madness. The scent of her arousal was intoxication. It made his cock throb painfully in his pants, but he struggled to control himself. He could not simply pounce on her like he wanted too without giving her time to come to grips with what they wanted from her. She needed time, and they would give it to her, because losing her now was not an option.

Oblivious to the brother's exchange, Alexis's nibbled on her lower lip as she felt a wave of arousal hit her like a meteor. Galan growled and the sound turned her on. She wanted him to do it again so she could feel that rumble in his chest that made her nipples tighten.

Shit, she needed to focus!

"So, if I take your blood, will I also be able to read your mind?"

"Aye, Alexis. You will have access to our thoughts and memories. You will also be able to call for us with just a thought if ever you need us."

The concept of blood bonding fascinating. With her empathic powers she was able to feel emotions, but how much easier would it be for her to be able to understand the feelings coming from them? Still, she wasn't naive enough to think that something like this was a decision to make on the spur of the moment. Mating with an alien race through blood was far more permanent than getting branded with a chosen mark on her face like humans did when forming a bonding unit.

This would be elemental…and forever.

"If I chose to mate with you I'm fine with the blood bond thing. Just…please give me a little time to decide. There is obviously some strong attraction between us, but this isn't something I can just jump into. It's a huge decision for me."

Elation surged through Galan, and he could feel the same satisfaction soothe Xavier's anger. His brother was a commanding force, and often forgot that a gentle touch sometimes got better results than demands. They might give her time, but there was no way they would let her go now that they found her. Alexis belonged to them, and they would do whatever it took to make sure she was mated to them when they left Earth. "Thank you, Alexis."

She blinked. "For what?"

"For considering mating with us. We know that it is a big decision, but we will make sure you never regret it."

She reached up to stroke his cheek and he could see the confusion in her beautiful violet eyes. "It's so strange. I just met you, but I feel like I know you."

Galan turned his head to nuzzle against her hand. Gods, he wanted her more than he'd ever wanted anything in his life. The feel of her in his arms felt so right, so perfect that he had to force himself not to just rip her clothing off and drag her to the floor where he could drive himself inside her. He wanted to take her, to slam himself so far into her that she would never be free of him.

"Your heart knows us. You were meant to belong to us and you honor us with your trust. We will not fail you."

Alexis' heart clenched hearing that. Most of the people in her past that she had depended on had let her down, but there was something about Xavier and Galan that made her want to trust them. She wanted to belong to them and to have them belong to her. It was absolutely crazy. None of this made sense, but it felt…like it was meant to be.

"I want you," she whispered, her voice shaking with nerves. "I do want all four of you, but I'm scared about what will happen…"

"Then let this be enough for now," Galan replied.

She nodded and watched as both of their silver eyes blazed with a hunger. Her breath caught as Galan's lips came down to meet hers, taking her in a soft, searing kiss that make her tremble. Alexis angled her head, needing to get closer to him and gasped as she felt Xavier come up behind her, reaching around to cup her full breasts in his large hands.

She lost herself in the kiss, immersing herself in the feel of them, loving their hands on her body. When she pulled back, she blinked in surprise as she suddenly realized that Xavier had removed her uniform top and bra while she had been busy kissing Galan. Her skin was flush with arousal, her nipples hard points that were aching to be touched.

As if sensing what she wanted, Galan lowered to his knees in front of her.

"These are perfect," he purred moving his head to suck her nipples. Her head fell back on Xavier's chest, trusting him to hold her up as Galan sucked on one nipple then switched to the other, lashing the taut bud with his tongue before sucking hard. She could feel each pull of his mouth like a lightning bolt that shot straight to her core. Xavier turned her head and settled his mouth over hers, forcing his tongue deep with a growl that made her weak with need.

They were taking her over and she let them. Galan's hands made quick work removing her boots then he went to work on her pants, also pulling her panties down her legs so she was standing naked between them.

"You are a vision, sweetling. A dream come true," Galan said reverently.

"Perfection," Xavier agreed with a rumbling purr. "I cannot wait to feel your beautiful body welcoming me inside you." Their words made her shiver and she gripped Xavier's head, pulling it back down to her so she could kiss him again.

More, she needed more.

Sharp hunger drove Alexis to rub her body back against Xavier, loving the feel of his steel- hard erection against her back. They were so much bigger than her, but she felt completely safe in their arms, sheltered between them. A gasp tore from her lips as Xavier lowered his hand between her legs, circling her clit with his finger.

Xavier drank down her moan as he pushed two fingers into her slick heat. She was dripping wet, and it pleased him to feel how much she wanted them. Never before had just seeing a female made his cock grow hard as stone. He let out a growl as he stared down at her beautiful body, running one of his hands over her lush curves and hips as he used his other to push his fingers inside her. His body trembled with need to take her…to bend her over the couch and ram his cock deep into her tight pussy until he filled her with his seed, but she wasn't ready yet. They were so much bigger than their tiny mate, and he knew his large cock would hurt her if she wasn't prepared to take him.

"So wet," Xavier purred against her ear. "Do you like the pleasure we are giving you, little one? Tell us. Tell us what you want, Alexis."

“Oh, god. I want you,” she panted, moaning as he began to finger fuck her faster as Galan went back to work sucking on her nipples. “Please, Xavier. Please…”

“You shall have us,” Xavier promised in a dark, heated growl. He wrapped his other arm around her middle, holding her back against him. “We will fill you so full you will not remember what it is like not to have us inside you, but first we need to make you come. Our cocks are large and we do not want to hurt you.”

“I have lube in a drawer by my bed in the other room,” she explained then winced at how that sounded. “Most relationships now are ménage so I’ve been with two men at—”

Both males snarled, cutting her off. “We do not want to hear about you with any other males. You belong to us now,” Xavier growled dangerously.

Alexis felt something inside of her shift. Normally, that kind of statement would have put her back up, but coming from them, it only enhanced her need. She wanted to belong to them. Everything they had said to her was like something out of her wildest fantasy. It was almost unimaginable how four strong Dragon Warriors would want someone like her when they could have anyone they wanted. She pushed that thought away, simply letting herself enjoy the moment as she ground her ass back against Xavier, making him suck in a harsh breath.

“Then take me,” she challenged.

“Aye, we will. First, we need to get your tight little pussy soft and slick with your cum to get you ready for us, little one. Come for us. Come and then we will take you.”

His fingers surged in and out of her pussy faster as the palm of his hand rubbed against her clit. Her body shuddered with her release as she exploded, her cream soaking Xavier’s hand as he curled his fingers to stroke the spot high inside her that made her damn toes curl.

She would have fallen, but they held her up between them. Closing her eyes, she let out a low moan as she rode the waves of ecstasy that wracked her body. Alexis had never come so fast and hard simply from being fingered before, but it didn't hurt that their fingers were the size of small cocks. That thought made a laugh slip past her lips and she realized she felt drunk with pleasure. She opened her eyes again and saw Galan standing before her completely naked, looking at her with such raw emotion her heart skipped a beat.

"I could listen to your laughter for the rest of days," Galan whispered softly, as if he meant it.

And he did…she could feel it.

She smiled as she looked at his gorgeous body. He was all hard muscles, covered with golden skin that practically glowed in the sunlight shining through the window. With his vest removed she could see that the dark gold and silver tattoos on his arms were actually covering most of his body. The intricate scrolling pattern started on the back of his hands, trailing up his arms and covered his shoulders and back then trailed down his sides to end at his hip bones. The design curled over the top half of his chest, almost looking like two dragons claws and she found the sight strangely arousing.

The dark lines made him look even more fierce, like the dark warrior that he was, but Alexis wasn't afraid. No, she was turned on to the point her body shuddered with need. Hoping she wasn't panting, she looked down and her jaw dropped when she saw Galan's massive cock jutting out from between his thighs.

Oh. My. God!

As an enhanced female she would normally be able to take a large dick with no problem, but Galan was huge! His impressive cock was thick and long and she could see the veins lining the hard column pulsing under the skin. The mushroomed head was larger than a humans, and the sight of him made her mouth water with the need to taste the pearly liquid seeping from the tip.

Damn, this might kill her, but what a way to go…

Always up for a challenge, she smiled at him and saw the flare of heat in his eyes as they burned brighter. She pushed him toward the couch, knowing full well she couldn't have moved him unless he let her. Once he was seated, that luscious, thick cock of his jutted out so it slapped against his stomach and the sight of it made her mouth water.

He held out a hand to her. "Come to me, my lady."

Alexis didn't hesitate. Stepping forward she climbed onto his lap so her legs were straddling him. She held onto his broad, muscular shoulders as she got into position, loving the way his biceps bulged as he moved. Leaning forward she captured his mouth again. Taking over, he ravaged her as he lifted her, settling her slick entrance over the head of his cock.

"Tell me you want me," Galan growled against her lips as he held her over his rock-hard cock that speared upward, ready to fuck. In response Alexis kissed him deep, thrusting her tongue into his mouth and wrapped her arms around his neck. He yanked her head back by her hair and looked into her violet eyes. "Tell me!"

The sharp bite of erotic pain had her moaning. "I want you, Galan."

Galan let out a loud groan against her mouth as he lowered her onto him. His cock slipped and slid over her glistening folds, but it didn't go in. Her hole was too small for the large head of his shaft to easily fit. Holding her easily in his arms, he moved her up and down, sliding her body on him so his shaft rubbed over her clit with each pass.

"Please," she moaned. "Stop teasing me! I want you inside me, now!"

His control snapped. Unable to wait any longer, he lodged the bulbous head of his cock to her pussy entrance and thrust his hips up hard. He let his magic flow out of him at the same time he pulled her body down on him, forcing his cock head inside her, stretching her wide.

Alexis cried out, her head falling back. Her body jolted as if she were electrocuted. Pleasure mixed with pain as his huge, hard length parted her.

My stars!

"My god, you're so fucking big!" she whimpered.

"Does it hurt?"

"Yes. No. I don't know…"

"Hold still, sweetling. Relax. I know you can take me, Alexis. Let my magic ease your body so it will open for me. I can ease you, but you have to let me in."

Alexis tried to relax her body so he could slide in further. He held completely still, allowing gravity to help her tight pussy take the thick column of his rock-hard cock slowly, at her own pace. She panted as she tried to take his impossibly massive length into her body then felt her body soften, aided by whatever magic he wielded.

She felt speared, filled to the max…and she loved it.

Galan was huge, and felt so good inside her. Clenching and releasing the tight muscles in her pussy, she slid down further on him and got an answering growl from Galan. The biting pain receded and pure pleasure filled her, making her want to move, to feel him sliding inside her.

Galan growled as he could feel her muscles flexing on his cock. She felt incredible, like he had just pushed into a secret haven made just for him that he never wanted to leave. It took all his strength to stay still, to allow her the time for her body to adjust to his penetration. He silently cursed himself for not licking her sweet pussy and bringing her to orgasm several more times before he attempted to take her, but he hadn't been able to wait any longer.

He needed her more than he needed air.

His cock felt harder than it had ever been before, and he sent more of his magic inside her to ease his passage into her heated depths. Stroking his tongue against hers, he held completely still as his magic softened her body for him. Long ago they had learned that they could lubricate their cocks or stretch a female channel with only a thought using their magic, allowing them to fuck a female with little effort on their part. Now that he had Alexis in his arms, he was grateful he had the ability more than he ever had been before.

He hated the pain he had caused her and fed more of his magic into her to help relax her body, allowing her to take him deeper until he was seated to the hilt. Her body softened, welcoming him inside as if she had been made for him. Her moans told him that there was no pain anymore and that only pleasure remained. He held her firmly as he began to move, gently rocking his cock up into her tight pussy.

"Better, sweetling?"

"Good, you feel so good," she moaned. She gave a little laugh. "My magic man."

"Male. I am no man. I am your male and hopefully will be your mate soon. Your perfect little pussy is gripping me so tight I could spill inside you just from filling you," Galan groaned. He flexed his hips, moving out then pushing deeper. "Hold on, Alexis. Just let me love you."

"Galan…"

Alexis squirm on him, wanting him to move faster, but he held her in place for his slow, measured thrusts. Their lips met, touching and tasting, sharing the beauty of the moment with one another. Knowing something was missing, she pulled back and turned her head to see Xavier standing naked, watching them. Silver eyes blazed down at her as he stroked his massive cock with his large hand. She was mesmerized at the sight of his hand working over his cock, and her mouth watered for a taste.

She smiled at him, feeling what his patience was costing him, and wanted him to be a part of this first time together. "Come here, Xavier. I want you in my mouth."

"You want to suckle me?" Xavier asked as he moved behind the couch, standing at the perfect height for her to suck on the large, thick length of him.

"Yes, I want to suck your cock. Is this okay?" she asked, pausing her movements on Galan as she looked at both of them in turn, not knowing how to proceed. She could feel the struggle inside Xavier, knowing that he was the more assertive one of the two brothers. He was showing her restraint as a sign that he would wait for her to decide whether or not she wanted to mate with them, and she fell a little further in love with him for that.

Galan's cock jerk inside her and he swiveled his hips under her. She squeezed her muscles on him again, making him growl in the way she loved so much and took that as his acceptance with bringing his brother into their play.

Xavier stepped forward. "Aye, Alexis. I would love to feel your hot little mouth on me."

Watching him, she reached out and took hold of his thick shaft in her small hand as Galan began to thrust inside her again. Xavier's glowing eyes stayed on hers as she moved her hand up and down his entire length. She could feel the waves of pleasure coming off of him mixing with the feelings she was getting from Galan so she was overwhelmed with their emotions. She tore her gaze away, looking down at Xavier's cock in amazement now that she got to look at him up close.

Stars, they were big...

Alexis could see that the mushroomed head of his cock was much larger than a humans, and there were three ridges right underneath the head. From the way Xavier's growls deepened when she stroked that area, she could tell it was a pleasure spot for him, and ruthlessly used it to her advantage. The shaft of his penis was so large there was no way she could close her hand around it, but she did her best with one hand while her other braced on Galan's shoulder for leverage. A pearly drop of liquid appeared at the tip of Xavier's cock, making her hungry for a taste.

With no hesitation, Alexis leaned forward to swipe at it with her tongue. The flavor of him exploded in her mouth, making her moan with pleasure. He was sweet and sinful, and tasted so good that the small drop only made her want more. Opening wide, she took the bulbous head into her mouth, sucking lightly, stroking her tongue over the ridges under his cock with her tongue and was rewarded with a spurt of pre-cum. Xavier snarled viciously as she worked her mouth over him, but his touch was gentle as he began stroking his hand over her hair.

"Alexis," Xavier snarled, making her look back up at him. His eyes were bright, glowing with the pleasure she was giving him. "Suck me, little one. Suck me deeper and keep your eyes on me," he ordered, taking command of their pleasure.

His body jerked as she moaned when Galan began sucking on her nipples. He worked her body over his erection faster, pushing her closer toward the brink of ecstasy. Lost in pleasure, she slid her mouth up and down Xavier, taking more of him into her mouth with each pass until she couldn't take anymore. She felt another burst of pre-cum shoot from Xavier's cock and drank it down greedily, letting the sweet flavor of him coat her throat.

God, the sweet taste of him was addicting.

Galan began thrusting faster, bracing his legs on the floor so he could begin pounding up inside her tight pussy harder. Just seeing Alexis with her mouth on his brother's cock had his own balls drawing up tight against his body, ready to spill his seed inside her, but not yet. Not until she came and took him with her. He wanted to show her how good they could make her feel, how good a mating would be between them. She was a true goddess, taking them both and sharing her pleasure with them freely, holding nothing back.

Reaching down between them, he stroked a finger over her clit, making her jolt as she slammed herself down on his cock in response.

"Fuck! I am going to spill. I cannot hold any longer," Galan growled out.

Hearing him, Alexis fisted Xavier's shaft harder and sucked desperately on his cock. She was so close, and wanted for all three of them to come together.

"Little one, pull back. Pull back unless you want to drink my seed down," Xavier growled out. She moaned, refusing to let go of her prize and kept stroking his cock as she sucked on him. Unable to hold back, his grip in her hair tightened as he roared out his release. "Mine!"

Alexis moaned as Xavier's semen shot down her throat in hard, heated spurts. The sweet taste of him had her own body clenching as it threw her into her own climax. Her eyes widened as she felt the base of Xavier's cock swell in her hand, growing larger so he had to use his own over hers to milk every last drop of his seed into her mouth.

Her body clamped down on Galan's thick cock, and she heard him curse as she felt the hot jets of his seed filling her pussy. She felt the same swelling in Galan's cock, this time in her pussy where it pushed at the sensitive nerve endings inside her. She came again, shuddering as wave after wave of pleasure hit her with the force of a meteor, leaving her breathless.

She collapsed against Galan as Xavier pulled back from her grip. She was immediately wrapped tight in Galan's protective embrace, his head buried in her neck as she rode out the aftershocks of her release.

"You are glorious, Alexis," he whispered in her ear. "And you belong to us."

A smile had her lips turning up as she rubbed her cheek against his shoulder, wanting to be as close to him as possible. Relaxing there in his arms, there was nowhere she would rather be. She could feel the waves of satisfaction coming from both males and knew she was in jeopardy of losing her heart to them. Not wanting to think about that yet, she laughed lightly. "Something you boys forgot to tell me?"

"Aye, our cocks swell when we come to ensure all of our seed stays inside you. Just relax, Alexis. The swelling has almost gone down."

Her smile disappeared as she realized what that meant for them…and her. Reminded of her flaw and what she could never have, some of her happiness died. "Well you guys don't have to worry about me getting pregnant or anything. I told you I was flawed."

Yelping, she was suddenly pulled off of Galan's cock and she found herself in Xavier's arms. "You will not say such things about yourself!" he growled. "No one is allowed to insult you, even you. You are not flawed, and it angers me greatly to hear you say it. If you mate with us we will be able to convert you to what we are, and you will bear us many younglings."

She was shocked speechless as he quickly carried her into her bedroom. How the hell was she supposed to respond to that? Could that really be possible?

Her eyes widened as he laid her down on the bed with his large frame covering her head to toe. His silver eyes were glowing with his fury as he glared down at her, but she wasn't scared. Strangely enough, she trusted him and it warmed her heart that he was angry on her behalf. Tears sparkled in her eyes as she dared to dream.

"I can't have children," she whispered, her throat tight.

Xavier's eyes softened and he leaned down to brush his lips against hers. "You may not as a human, but you will be able to with us."

She gasped as Xavier spread her legs wide with his and he pushed inside her in one quick thrust, filling her completely. "Wh-what?"

"I need inside your sweet pussy, little one. I am sorry, but I cannot wait," Xavier said in a strangled voice that sounded pained.

"Already? But you just came!"

"I am still hard and hurting for you. I need to fill you with my seed and claim you as mine," Xavier growled. The thought of her swollen with their younglings had him so hard that it hurt. He wanted to fuck himself into her, over and over again until she was so full of him she would never be the same. He wanted to change her, the need so strong it sang through his bloodstream like a compulsion, but he forced himself to wait.

He held still, fully embedded inside her so the head of his cock was pressed up against the entrance of her womb and ground his hips into her, wanting to be as deep inside her as he could get. Fuck, she felt so good he wanted to spend the rest of his days right there with the two of them connected. It infuriated him to think of anyone considering her flawed when she was perfect to them. When she agreed to be their mate, they would convert her into a dragon shifter through a blood bond and infuse her with their magic. Her body would be changed, altered so that anything wrong inside of her would be healed.

Alexis' hand came up to stroke his cheek and she smiled. She could feel how much he needed her, and it filled her with happiness. "Then don't stop," she whispered, drawing his head down for a kiss. "Let me give you what you need."

Pushing all thoughts aside, Alexis focused on the now as he used his knees to push her thighs wider, spreading her open for him and his lips took hers in a brutal kiss. Her breath caught as he surged inside her, not stopping as he began thrusting into her with a punishing rhythm that absolutely thrilled her. Her hands slid over his sweat-soaked skin, tracing the corded muscles of his back then back up to his wide shoulders, needing something to hold on as his cock filled her over and over again.

She tore her mouth from his as she saw Galan sitting next to them, stroking his cock as he watched. “Wait, Xavier…”

Xavier paused, his large body shaking with the need to move. She could feel the barely restrained power humming in his massive body, but he did as she asked.

“I need—”

Alexis pressed a finger to his lips to still the plea that tore from his lips. “I want you both. Together.”

She watched as Xavier’s eyes glowed brighter, felt him grow impossibly harder inside her as she felt the waves of their lust flooding her system. In that moment she knew she had made the right decision. Sure, she was a little intimidated by taking both of their cocks inside her at once, but she felt that they needed this, and to be honest, so did she.

“You want both of us to take you together?” Xavier asked.

“I…I do.”

“Then you shall have us.”

Xavier quickly rolled them over on the bed so she was on top of him, straddling his hips. He held her down on his cock and spread her legs wider for Galan to get behind her. Holding her to him, Xavier slowly pushed his dick deep, pausing when he was buried to the hilt inside her. “Relax and let us pleasure you, Alexis. Let us love you together.”

“Umm,” she whispered nervously. “I do want this, but you guys are pretty damn big. I think we need to use some lube or something.”

“Remember,” Galan whispered in her ear as he bent over her from behind. “We are your magic males. Trust us. We would never hurt you.”

Alexis held still as she felt Galan slowly swirling the head of his cock through the liquid coated her sex from their earlier play.

She braced herself on Xavier, waiting for the burn that was to come, but still couldn't help but gasp as she felt Galan press a finger into her. The single digit sank into her then he added a second to stretch her wider, preparing her.

"Shh, little one. Just relax and let us make you ours," Xavier purred to her as he pressed soft kisses to her lips. "Let Galan in and we shall love you as you have never been loved before."

Galan barely held onto his control as he pulled his fingers out of her and pressed the large head of his cock to the tight rosebud of her ass. Pushing gently he tried to enter her, but she was so damn tight that her body fought his penetration. By the goddess, he wanted to shove his cock deep inside her, but knew he had to take it slow or he would hurt her, magic or not. He closed his eyes and focused on using his powers to help her body yield to him and felt himself slowly slide into her hot little hole.

"That is it," Xavier whispered softly as he stayed still, his cock buried to the hilt inside her pussy. "Hold onto me and let Galan work his cock up your ass. Let us take you, mate."

Alexis shivered as Xavier called her his mate. Hearing that word and the depth of meaning he put into it made her want them to claim her for real. She fought the desire to tell them to just claim her and to hell with her reservations. No, she couldn't do that…not yet. She breathed out long and hard as Galan pushed his massive cock into her ass so slowly she felt every ridge sliding across the sensitive tissue inside her.

"By the goddess, she is tight!" Galan gasped.

"Tight," Xavier snarled. "So tight, and ours!"

Xavier's arms wrapped around her, holding her against his chest as Galan slowly thrust his long cock into her ass so it rubbed against his own through the thin membrane that separated them. It felt so good, like they were finally where they were meant to be. He kissed her, drinking down her moans as Galan worked himself into her and fought the urge to sink his fangs inside her so he could bind them together forever.

"You were made for us," Galan purred into her ear as he rocked his cock inside of her, forging deeper each time. "This is what awaits you as our mate. The ultimate pleasure. We can give you this every time. Do you want that? Do you want us moving inside you, giving you everything you need?"

"Yes, oh god yes!"

Xavier and Galan's eyes met and Alexis screamed out incoherently as they began fucking her, working in tandem. Galan pulled back and slammed his hips against her ass, forcing his cock deep inside her while Xavier pulled out. When he slammed up, Galan pulled back in perfect unison, working her body like two maestros.

Alexis lost her ability to speak as both males filled her with their enormous cocks. Riding high on her own pleasure, it was intensified by both Xavier and Galan's elation of being with her. The feeling of both her lovers taking her together was unlike anything she had ever experienced before. Sure, she had been fucked by two men before, but it had been nothing like this. This wasn't just fucking…it was as if their souls were merging. She was pure sensation, and her empathic powers were making it feel like they were one being. She threw her head back and moaned as Xavier and Galan began thrusting faster, slamming one cock in as the other pulled out.

"Your pleasure belongs to us." Xavier gripped his hand in Alexis's hair, positioning her so his mouth could savage hers.

"You need what we can give you, Alexis. Tell us. Let us give you what you need," Galan growled.

"I need you," Alexis sobbed, unable to hold the words back as her body tightened.

“Come for us, little one,” Xavier demanded as he held her to him. “Let us care for you and you will want for nothing. Come for us now!”

Alexis screamed out as her body shattered, locking down on both of them. Galan jerked his cock from her ass, and she heard his low growl as his hot seed splashed on her back, coating her skin with his release. Seconds later, Xavier let out a roar as he climaxed inside her, his cock swelling as he filled her with pulse after pulse of his hot semen.

The feeling of Xavier swelling inside her triggered another hard climax, even more intense than the first and had Alexis screaming so loud her throat was hoarse. Shudders racked her body and her vision blurred. She heard both Xavier and Galan’s soft voices crooning to her and smiled blissfully as she let herself drift off into the darkness.

Death by sex…what a way to go.

Chapter Five

So, this is what hell is like...

Alexis was more miserable then she could ever recall being as she sat at the table of a lavish meal in one of the most decadent restaurants in the Capital. Not that she could really appreciate the amazing food she had been served since she'd only taken a couple of bites.

Surrounded by several regents, commanders, and other guests, Alexis couldn't concentrate on any of the conversations going on around her. She was being bombarded by emotions from everyone at the table, and it was difficult not to get overwhelmed by all of the various sensations she was feeling. Actually, she had passed being overwhelmed fifteen minutes ago.

Now, she was simply screwed.

Usually able to control her gift, it was alarming that she couldn't seem to get a handle on everything going on around her. All of her senses seemed to be amplified, making it impossible to filter out the waves of emotions she was getting from everyone at the table. Her head hurt from the constant bombardment, and she had a sick feeling in the pit of her stomach that destroyed any appetite she'd had, even after the strenuous activities she had participated in earlier.

This afternoon she had opened herself up more than she ever had before...even with her past relationships. Being with Xavier and Galan had felt so right, like it had been fated for her to meet them and she knew that she had already given them a piece of her heart. No matter how foolish she'd told herself it was after knowing them for only a day it was as if her soul had recognize theirs.

That is why it hurt so much when they had pulled away from her.

When they had returned to the visitors suite with a bag of her belongings, Xavier and Galan had stepped back, leaving her to struggle with her own feelings. Logically, she knew that they had been giving her time to get to know Thorn and Brydan, but she couldn't help but feel like they had abandoned her after they had gotten what they wanted from her. Like they once they had fucking tagged the other team, she was no longer their problem to deal with.

After they had finished making love on her bed, she had briefly passed out from the pleasure. When she woke, Xavier and Galan were stroking her with their large hands. Not to arouse, but to comfort and soothe. They had made her feel cherished, and it was something that she wasn't used to, but she could really learn to appreciate. They had taken a shower together, but since is wasn't big enough for any more playtime, they'd simply washed and headed back to the visitors suite just in time for her to get settled then head out to the dinner that was being hosted by the regents. Not wanting to be seen escorting them around town out of uniform before that evening, she had put on a fresh uniform and packed away her outfit for dinner along with her other belongings.

Back at the visitors suite, Thorn and Brydan had joined her in the room she had chosen for her own use while she was staying with them as she unpacked. Thorn had been courteous and Brydan had a wicked wit that made her laugh, but neither of them had made any advances toward her or shown her that they wanted to mate with her like Xavier and Galan had.

The change in the dynamics had left her shaky and slightly bewildered. When Xavier and Galan had simply disappeared after handing her over, it hurt. Thorn and Brydan's disinterest had compounded that hurt and began turning it into a bitter anger that she'd thought she would never feel again. She held back the words that had wanted to spew out, unsure if she was gauging the situation accurately or if she was simply letting past betrayals taint the present.

All four of the Dragon Warriors had looked amazing after they had changed for the dinner. Xavier and Galan had chosen to wear dark blue shirts, while Thorn and Brydan wore white with their black leather pants. The shirts were made of a shimmering fabric Alexis had never seen before. She'd wanted to reach out and touch it, but she'd felt awkward doing so after the distance she felt between them.

Alexis had changed into a beautiful ombre dress the color of a pale lavender that darkened to a deep indigo toward the bottom and she'd left her hair down for the occasion. It wasn't often that she had the opportunity to dress in civilian clothing and she wanted to take full advantage. Hell, who was she kidding? She wanted to impress all four of the Dragon Warriors, and had been secretly pleased with their reactions when they saw her after she stepped from her room. The lust coming off all four males had left her weak in the knees, but it had mystified her greatly when none of them had made a move to touch her before they left.

Now, sitting at the table surrounded by people, she couldn't seem to get a handle on what the hell was going on and it was making her crazy. Seated in between Thorn and Brydan, with Xavier and Galan sitting across the table from her, she couldn't look anywhere without seeing one of them.

Not that she wanted to look at any of them at the moment.

She was furious at Xavier and Galan about their behavior earlier, and the heated looks they kept sending her from across the table made her want to slap them both. When her friend Sullivan Archer, Jax's second-in-command, had directed a flirtatious comment at her before they were seated, Xavier had actually snarled at him. Thank god no one else had heard him, but Archer had been casting suspicious glances at the Dragon Warriors throughout dinner.

Discretion was obviously something neither Xavier nor Galan was familiar with, and Alexis was sure everyone was going to know what had happened between them from the way they were looking at her. To make matters worse, there was a fire tearing through her that bordered on pain, making her pussy weep with her juices as if she was nothing more than a mass of raging hormones. Each time they looked at her it was as if she felt it like a physical caress, and her womb clenched as she remembered how it felt when they had been deep inside her.

Damn them for making her want them so much even when she wanted to kill them.

It didn't help to focus on her other dinner companions either. To Alexis' right, Brydan was using his sharp wit to entertain several of the dinner guests, practically turning his back to Alexis completely. On her left, Thorn's attention was being monopolized by the very beautiful, very unclaimed Scroll, Marianna Dexter. Marianna was one of the regents' daughters and also one of the most coveted women in the Capital. Alexis was forced to sit there listen as the Scroll flirted outrageously with Thorn, and she could barely restrain herself from jumping out of her chair and attacking the other woman.

She had never felt so out of control or so humiliated.

This wasn't like her. Eaten alive by jealousy, she didn't feel like herself. Closing her eyes for a moment, she took a deep breath to steady herself, but when she opened them back up she felt her temper flare as Marianna reach out and touch Thorn's arm.

Oh, hell no…

Alexis stopped the pretense of eating and set her fork down on her plate, pushing it away from herself before she stabbed the bitch with it. She knew she had to get out of there before she did something she would regret, and maybe get her ass thrown in prison. Needing a moment alone to get herself together before she exploded, she stood up.

Xavier, Galan, Thorn and Brydan immediately stood, as did all the other men, but she quickly gestured for them to take their seats again. She caught Jax's gaze and focused on her commander to steady herself, noting the concern in his eyes.

"Everything okay, Lex?"

"Sorry, I'm not feeling well. Please, excuse me for a minute."

She excused herself from the table, and could feel four sets of glowing eyes on her as she left without looking at any of them. The emotions swirling around inside her were driving her insane. One second she wanted nothing more than to jump them to sate the need burning inside her then the next she wanted to punch them in their stupid faces for pissing her off. Neither was a viable option at the moment since the very last thing she wanted to do was make a fool of herself in front of her commanders and the regents, so she forced herself to restrain her temper until she was alone.

Damning herself and feeling like a fool, she hurried down the hallway, out onto the empty balcony, away from the Dragon Warriors and their empty promises. She brushed furiously at the tears sliding down her cheeks then tipped her head back to allow the cool breeze to dry her eyes before any more escaped.

She had actually let herself start to believe all the shit they had told her early, about wanting her for a mate and being able to change her so she could have children. At the time she had been so overwhelmed with the combination of her lust and their emotions that she hadn't been able to really think about everything they had told her about the mating and what it meant for the future.

It still all seemed so fantastical that it couldn't be real. It wasn't every day that four mysterious strangers came to Earth and granted her greatest wish, especially when they looked like Xavier, Galan, Thorn and Brydan.

She'd thought they were too good to be true…and clearly she had been right.

Alexis let out a gasp as she was whirled around and found herself staring into Thorn's beautiful, glowing golden eyes. Her hands reached out to grip his strong biceps trying to keep some distance between them, but he pulled her closer.

"Why do you weep, love? What ails you?"

"Let me go," Alexis ordered as she tried to shove him away. It was like trying to move a mountain and did no good, but it didn't mean she would give up. The gentle tone of his voice was enough to make the tears fall faster and she hated the fact that she wanted to burrow closer to his warmth to seek comfort. Feeling like an idiot, she struggled to break free of his hold on her.

"Nay, Alexis. I will not release you until you tell me what is wrong."

His panic and concern made her laugh, but it was void of all humor. She felt heartsick that he could act like he cared about what she was feeling after how he had been behaving earlier. Fine. He really wanted to know what was bothering her?

Then she'd fucking tell him.

"You want to know what's wrong? How 'bout asking what *isn't* wrong? Why don't you stop with the bullshit concern, or are you going to milk that until you get laid too?"

Alexis watched his head rear back as if she slapped him, his glowing golden eyes wide with alarm. She instantly felt contrite for the words she had spoken, but her pain had caused her to lash out. It took a few seconds for him to process what she just said then his eyes narrowed in rage.

Fine, fuck it. She quit anyways.

If he wanted to be mad at her then let him. At least they would both be miserable now.

"That was unfair, Alexis." Galan said softly from behind her. "I can feel your pain as if it were my own and we aren't even mated yet. Do not strike out at us for being concerned for you."

"Oh, like you were concerned earlier when you just handed me over to your friends after you got what you wanted?" Alexis said with a harsh laugh as she yanked her arms free of Thorn, who had frozen in shock. She rounded on them, looking at both males and not bothering to hide the hurt and anger she felt. "Sure, you and Xavier got fucked all afternoon so why bother having to talk to me when you were trying to make sure your buddies got some next?"

"It was not like that," Galan growled, his silver eyes flashing with fury.

"Then tell me how exactly I was supposed to take it, Galan. Silly me, when I thought you were being serious about wanting me to be your mate. Would a mate leave a woman after she slept with them, when she was struggling to understand what the hell just happened? Tell me, would he really push her off on someone else to take care of?"

Alexis watched the blood drain from Galan's face and she saw his pained expression as she moved out of reach when he tried to touch her. "Is that what you thought? It was not like that, sweetling. Xavier and I had you all afternoon. It was only fair to allow Thorn and Brydan to spend some time with you."

Could they really be that stupid?

She shook her head. "Oh yeah, because Thorn and Brydan supposedly want to mate with me too, not that I can tell by their actions." She turned to glare at Thorn. She knew she was being overly emotional, but she couldn't seem to help the words spewing from her mouth. They had fucking hurt her. All four of them had and it was killing her for them to stand there and look at her like she was being unreasonable.

"Why the hell did you bother sitting next to me if you and your brother were going to ignore me all night? If you are going to flirt with another woman, fine, I don't own you. But don't you dare tell me you want to be in a relationship with me when you can't even show me a little courtesy!"

"I was not flirting! I would not do that to you, Alexis," Thorn growled heatedly. "And we are in a relationship! We want you for our mate!"

“Whatever.” Alexis whispered sadly, not believing him. “You have a strange fucking way of showing it then.”

Damn, she wanted to go back in time. To start the evening over from the moment they had left her living quarters earlier. If she could she would have never allowed herself to believe that the four of them really wanted her.

She would have never dared to dream…

“You asked us not to allow your colleagues to know about what we are to you until you decided to mate with us, so that is what we were doing,” Thorn growled from behind her. She spun around and saw him standing there with his hands fisted, his golden eyes bright with condemnation.

Well, fuck him very much.

Not wanting them to out her in front of the regents and her commander meant they were free to flirt with whoever they wanted? “So this was all to get back at me for not wanting my commanders to know until I made my decision? Excuse me for worrying about losing my job! Are you really telling me there wasn’t something in between Xavier and Galan eye fucking me from across the table and you and Brydan ignoring me?”

Suddenly, she was very tired. Sitting down on a stone bench, she turned away from them. “Please leave. I don’t want to talk to either of you right now.”

“Alexis—”

“Please, Galan,” she said, her voice strained with unshed tears as her vision blurred, but she didn’t let them fall. Not yet. “I really don’t want to do this here. If you care about me at all you will leave me to get my shit together before I have to go back in there and salvage what is left of this farce.”

She held her breath and finally released it as she heard the door softly open and shut again. Closing her eyes again she wrapped her arms around herself for comfort and rocked a little. It was a habit she had learned when she was young. With no one to hold her and comfort her, she had learned to depend on herself. Later when she had met Draven and Cristof, she'd thought she had finally found someone to care about her, but she had been very wrong. They had taken her trust and used her for their own purposes. She hadn't mattered to them and swore she would never allow herself to be treated like that again.

Obviously, she was wrong on a fucking epic level.

Giving in to the tears that wanted to come, she put her hands over her face and let them spill down her cheeks unheeded.

"Alexis…my love."

She gasped as she was caught up in strong arms. Thorn said her name in such a tortured voice it hurt her heart. Damn it, she thought he had gone back inside with Galan. He pulled her onto his lap as he sat down on the floor.

"Do not fight me, please," he whispered as he buried his face into her neck, cradling her against him. "We never wanted to make you feel unwanted. You are the mate of my heart already, no matter that you have not allowed us to claim you. I vow it is true."

The sincerity in his voice gave her pause and she stopped struggling against him, allowing her body to relax against his powerful frame as he sheltered her in his arms.

"It took everything in me to sit there and behave," Brydan hissed out softly, his voice shaking with emotions. Alexis looked up in surprise to where he was sitting on the bench. It shocked her that she hadn't heard him come out and join them, but then again she had been distracted bawling her eyes out like a child.

"What do you mean?" she asked, trying to pull herself together.

"I could not look at you," Brydan said after huffing out an impatient breath. He rubbed his hands over his thick thighs and glared at her. "Do you think it is easy having felt the pleasure you gave Xavier and Galan this afternoon then to restrain ourselves while we gave you time to get comfortable in our presence?"

Holy hell.

She gasped. "You…felt what we did?"

"Aye, we did. And it took all our will not to just throw you down on the bed and take you like they did when you returned to our quarters," Brydan growled as he looked at her through narrowed eyes. "Then we had to attend this damned dinner because you wanted us to. If I looked at you I would have dragged you out of that room and taken you against the wall. Did you want that, Alexis?"

She couldn't even form the words to respond as she gaped at him. The vicious snarl on his face didn't scare her. Instead, she felt something that had broken inside her begin to mend. Thorn's arms were wound tight around her, holding her close to him as if he wanted to merge their bodies together if he could.

Communication was a bitch in a normal relationship, and even more so when trying to navigate the current minefield she found herself in, not to mention that her emotions seemed to be going haywire. She felt appeased now that Brydan and Thorn had explained their actions a bit, but she wouldn't, couldn't allow them to treat her in a way that made her feel bad about herself, no matter if it had been a misunderstanding.

Perhaps she had overreacted, but it wasn't as if she could help how she felt.

"You…all of you made me feel cheap earlier, and tonight at dinner made me think that I couldn't count on any of you the way I thought I could," Alexis explained softly, wanting them to understand her reaction.

Thorn's arms tightened around her, practically squeezing her to death, but she didn't complain. "We never wanted to make you feel like that."

"I know that now," Alexis sighed as she let herself relax against him. "I'm sorry if I overreacted, but…I can feel the emotions of everyone at the table, especially the women that the four of you are talking to. I can also sense your lust—"

"It is only for you," Brydan swore with such vehemence that she couldn't help but believe him.

It was humiliating, but she knew they deserved to know about her past. Taking a deep breath, she let it out and said, "I got out of a really bad relationship where the men treated me as if I wasn't good enough. They wanted me in private, but in public, they treated me like you did tonight."

She watched Brydan wince and felt Thorn do the same. Thorn growled low in his throat in a sound so raw it both thrilled her and terrified her. "Who are these males? We will end them for you for ever making you feel like that."

A small chuckle escaped. "That's sweet…and slightly disturbing. But I don't need you to take care of them. I ended it and moved on. I'm simply telling you this because I have some issues with the men I'm supposed to be with ignoring me in public. It makes me feel—"

"Never again will you feel anything less than wanted and cared for in our presence," Thorn swore after he turned her head so he was looking down at her with somber, glowing eyes. "You are too important for us not to give you what you need."

Alexis' hand lifted to grab hold of his thick wrist. "What about what you need?"

Fire flashed in his eyes then they dulled again to a muted glow. She could feel the sadness coming off him in waves and she immediately wanted to do whatever she could to ease the ache she felt inside him. "You are not ready to mate with us."

She didn't know about that. It was crazy how possessive she felt about them already after knowing them such a short time. She'd wanted to kill the other women speaking to them, and suspected that it would be that way as long as she knew them. Her free hand clenched into a fist. Just the thought of any of them being with someone else made her want to…

Hell, just thinking about them leaving and never seeing them again had pain surging through her so acute it stole her breath.

Jesus, she felt like she was losing her mind!

Her body was shaking with all the swirling emotions careening inside her. She needed to get her shit together or she thought she was going to implode. She let out a gasp as she was hauled out of Thorn's arms and found herself staring into Xavier's furious silver eyes. Both Xavier and Galan had stormed back out onto the balcony, and she could feel the waves of their lust and anger fueling her own.

"Enough! This pain you are feeling is unnecessary. We want only you. It has been unbearable for my brother and I to hold ourselves back and give you time. I was moments away from throwing you down on the table and taking you in front of everyone because all of those males do not know who you belong to, and yet you question how much we want you?" he growled furiously. "You are mine!"

"Calm, Xavier," Thorn warned in a low voice.

Xavier snarled at him. "I will not have our mate questioning our loyalty to her!"

"She is not yet our mate," Brydan reminded him

"I am not so sure about that," Galan said softly. "I am bound to her already. I feel it."

"As am I," Xavier growled with conviction.

Alexis' eyes widened. "But I…you…how is that possible?"

"I do not know, but this would explain the jealousy and hurt you were feeling. Our race feels deeply, much more than humans. If we had a blood bond with you we would have been able to feel what you did, just as you would feel us," Galan explained passionately. "You would never have reason to doubt our feelings for you."

"You have no need for doubt, Alexis. I am already mated to you, blood bond or not. I feel you here." Xavier put his hand over his heart. “I know you needed time, but I have already claimed you. You belong to me…to us, and we will not let you go.”

Alexis felt the surge of emotions emanating from them. Somehow she could tell that all four of them were furious at themselves, but mixed with that was a feeling of satisfaction and a deep sense of pride that she was theirs. Yes, they’d hurt her, but she had hurt them as well, by doubting their feelings for her and refusing their claim. She knew they were waiting for her to explode, to scream at them and unleash her fury for taking away her choice…but she wasn’t angry.

Instead, she felt free.

She could feel their sincerity and had never felt more ashamed of her gifts than now. Since meeting them she had been reading their emotions, reacting automatically to how they were feeling, but she had been denying them that same right.

Logic had been holding her back, telling her it was too soon to make a monumental decision that would affect the rest of her life. She’d only just met them, yet in her heart she felt like she’d been waiting for them her whole life. Like they were the missing pieces of her she had never even known were missing until she saw them.

Normally, she didn’t like taking chances. She was a planner, and liked to know what to expect before she did anything new, but nothing about this was expected. How the hell could she have planned meeting four alien warriors that could shift into dragons that would want to claim her as their mate?

Alexis wasn’t anything special, but the way they looked at her made her feel like the most beautiful woman in the world…hell, in the entire galaxy. When she felt their emotions it was as if they were a part of her.

When they touched her, she shivered.

When they looked at her, she melted.

Knowing they’d claimed her settled something inside of her that had been aching. It meant that she belonged, when she never had before…not really. It also meant that they belonged to her, and that she would never lose them. Mating was a bond stronger than anything humans could imagine, and she wanted that with them.

Alexis didn't give a damn about waiting any longer, and she knew what they said was true. In her heart she was already their mate. The scent of Xavier's skin was like an aphrodisiac to her already overloaded senses. His snarls didn't scare her. In fact, it made her hot, so hot she couldn't control herself, and she stopped trying. Gripping his hair, she surprised him as she crushed her mouth to his in a searing kiss.

His taste exploded on her tongue, and it made her want to devour him in big, greedy bites. He immediately responded in kind, taking control of their kiss as he plundered her mouth. She loved how commanding he was and moaned at the pleasure he gave her.

Xavier pulled back, breathing hard. His eyes burning a molten silver as he looked down at her and she shivered at the intensity in his gaze. "Does this mean you are not angry any longer?"

She slowly smiled. "No, I'm not. Actually, I'm relieved. It might be sooner than I had planned, but I think the outcome was inevitable. I couldn't give you up. Any of you. I want to be your mate. Actually, I feel like I already am."

"You are," he growled.

"She may be claimed by you, but not by us. Not yet," Thorn said, his voice dark with need. "And we are going to fix that…right now."

Chapter Six

In the time it took Alexis to blink she found herself teleported back in the living room of the guest suite with her four Dragon Warriors. Their magic sure came in handy and was a pretty damn slick mode of transportation.

"Wow, now that is a cool trick."

Xavier chuckled. "Glad I could please you, mate."

"Come here, my love," Thorn commanded as he took her from Xavier's arms, carrying her into her bedroom that she had taken in the guest suite.

Exhilarated, Alexis let out a laugh. "I am going to have a hell of a time explaining all this to my commander tomorrow."

"You should not have to answer to any other male regarding out mating," Xavier growled. She rolled her eyes at him. Somehow she had known he was going to say that.

"We shall just have to make it worth your while then," Brydan said, his eyes sparkling with mirth. Thorn set her back on her feet and she shivered as Brydan lowered the zipper of her dress, stroking his fingers along her naked back. He turned her to look at him.

"I need you. Are you ready to mate with us, Lexie?" Brydan asked. "Blood bond and all, or are we rushing you?"

Concern warred with desire, making her hesitate for a moment. She couldn't deny that she was still nervous about making such a permanent commitment to them, but the alternative wasn't an option. Just thinking about losing them made her heart ache and she never wanted to find out what that would feel like in reality.

Taking a deep breath, she took the plunge and winked at him. "I guess that's only fair since I can read your emotions." She wrapped her arms around his waist when she saw his glowing eyes dim and felt his disappointment. Decision made, she gifted them all with a serious smile. "I was kidding, Brydan. I would be honored to mate with you fully. I want to be yours. I feel…I know we've only just met, but I'm ready to be your mate."

Brydan stroked his hand down her cheek, loving the feeling of her soft skin as he saw sincerity shimmering in her beautiful violet eyes. He pushed her dress down, letting it fall to the floor so she was wearing nothing but a tiny scrap of material that hid her pussy from him. His eyes narrowed at the offending barrier and took hold of it, tearing it from her with one pull.

She laughed. "You could have just asked me to take it off."

"I liked my way better," Brydan said with a low growl and he took off her wrist unit and dropped it onto the floor onto her dress. She was sheer perfection and he could hardly believe that she was willing to give herself to them. "You are so beautiful."

"I feel beautiful when you look at me."

He leaned down and kissed her sweetly, stroking her tongue with his own, pulling her body up against his. Sitting next to her at dinner without being able to touch her had been torture. He'd barely been able to eat, intoxicating by the scent of her need. It had driven him crazy not being able to hear what she was thinking, and the scent of her pain had made him lose his mind.

He had done his best to hold a conversation with the other people at the table, but he had wished them all to hell for taking time that could have been spent alone with her. Knowing that Xavier and Galan had already claimed her made him crazy with the need to take her, to sate his lust within her body and form a bond that could never be broken so that no one could ever take her from them.

Thorn moved up behind them, pressing against Alexis' back as he kissed her neck. He loved how she leaned back against him, and he felt his cock harden to the point of pain as he imagined taking her ass while his brother fucked her pussy. He could feel the depth of emotion his brother felt for their little mate, and it matched his own. Alexis was every wish, every dream he had ever had, and she was finally going to be theirs.

Forever.

By the gods, he was shaking with the need to take her. Hunger tore through him, making him feel feral. Never had he wanted a female so much he thought he would go mad if he didn't claim her. Just the sound of her laughter had his dick swelling so he was hard and aching. He wanted to throw her back onto the bed, spread her wide and mount her. Ride her until he spilled himself deep in her pussy, and bind her to him so she would never be free of them.

Thorn made a silent vow that he would always show her that she'd made the right choice, that she would never regret binding her life to theirs. He would never fail her, and he would love her to the end of days.

Turning his head he glanced over at Xavier and Galan, noticing that both of his friends were tense. *"Will you be able to wait while we bond with her?"* Thorn asked through their blood bond.

"Aye, we will take her after you do, but hurry," Xavier replied.

Thorn could feel the urgency they felt that matched his own and knew they couldn't wait much longer. He knew that waiting would be harder for Xavier, since he was the most demanding of all of them, but what surprised him the struggle he felt inside Galan. He could feel that it was costing them both to stand back and let Thorn and Brydan have their time with Alexis, and he appreciated it greatly. He didn't want to have to fight the brothers of his heart, and knew he was close to violence if anyone challenged him right now.

Before he could say anything else, Alexis broke away from Brydan and turned to look up at him with concern. She stroked his cheek, and by the goddess, her soft hand on his face felt amazing. He rubbed himself against it, imagining how her tiny hand would feel stroking over his entire body and felt his cock pulse in his pants, straining to break free.

"Where did you go?" she whispered softly.

Not wanting any untruths between them, Thorn answered honestly. "I was speaking to Xavier through our bond. They need you as much as Brydan and I do and asked that we move this along."

The smile she gifted him with warmed his heart. "So, you really can speak to each other in your minds? That's pretty cool."

"Aye, and soon you will be able to do the same. I do not mean to rush you, but we are barely holding on to our control. We need to mate with you, Alexis. We need to form the blood bond with you while we are deep in your body and claim you as our own."

Alexis' eyes went wide and her breathing sped up. "Then don't wait. I'm ready."

He growled as he crushed his mouth back down on hers, feasting on her sweet taste. When he pulled back he saw that Brydan had shed his clothing and was sitting down on the bed.

"Come here, Lexie."

Alexis felt her heart pound as she looked at Brydan. Stars, he looked like some sort of golden god sitting there. All four males were gorgeous. With tight, roped muscles beneath golden skin, Brydan looked like her wildest fantasy come to life. She held back a laugh. Hell, this *was* a fantasy. Where else would she ever find four hot males who wanted to mate with her?

Both Brydan and Thorn were slightly shorter than Xavier and Galan, but they were also broader, heavier with dense muscle. Brydan's long, thick cock jutted out in front of him, pointing straight out like it was reached toward her. She could see a drop of pre-cum leaking from the slit and lust surged through her so strong that it made her knees go weak. She had never felt so wild with the need to fuck, to feel a man moving over her, in her. Her pussy clenched at the thought, and she knew if she didn't get one of them inside her soon she would go mad, but first she wanted to taste Brydan.

Standing there, Alexis was surprised that she didn't feel the least bit self-conscious being naked in front of all four of them. Instead, it made her feel powerful that all four males wanted her so much. She could feel their desire for her through her gift and it eased the part of her that had been hurting before.

No, desire was too tame a word for what they felt.

They *needed* her.

Through her peripheral vision she could see that Thorn, Xavier and Galan were all tearing off their own clothes, and smiled at their jerky movements. Focusing back on Brydan, she stepped forward and stopped him before he could lift her. He gave her a questioning look and she smiled at him then bent over at the waist, spreading her legs as she kept them straight. Dressed in nothing more than her high heels she could imagine the view she was giving the others, putting her dripping pussy on display.

Satisfaction surged through her as all three of the males behind her growled and groaned. Yeah, they wanted her alright, and feeling their yearning for her took away the last sliver of doubt and gave her courage. Giving in to her desire, she licked at the pearl of pre-cum seeping from the head of Brydan's cock and hummed in pleasure as he let out a vicious growl. He went still beneath her and she looked up to see his golden eyes burned with a new intensity so bright that it took her breath away.

"You taste so sweet," she whispered, licking her lips to enjoy the taste of him.

"Fuck! Take me into your sweet, little mouth, Lexie. Let me feel you suckle from me."

Doing as he asked, she opened wide, stretching so she could take him into her mouth, and was rewarded as he let out another growl. She loved the sounds they all made, letting her know they liked what she was doing. She began sliding up and down Brydan's thick length as she used her hands to hold the base of his cock that she couldn't take. The waves of emotions coming off of him grew stronger, until she was as desperate for release as he was.

"By the gods, her hot, little mouth is so sweet and hot."

"It is," Xavier said as he sat down on the bed, watching them intently. "She had me shooting my seed straight down her throat. Just wait until you feel our mate's tight pussy welcoming you inside her."

God, their dirty talk had her pussy dripping even more and she moaned as two thick fingers rubbed at the slickness pouring from her core.

"She is so wet for us," Thorn growled out from behind her, his voice tight with need.

She gasped as he thrust his fingers into her pussy, rubbing against the sensitive tissue inside her, but it wasn't enough. She felt out of control, wild with a lust she couldn't contain any longer. The entire night had been like foreplay and she was done being teased. She felt empty and the ache inside her just seemed to grow stronger. She pulled off Brydan's cock, looking up at him in confusion. "I don't know what's wrong with me. I want you so fucking bad I'm about to lose my mind."

Brydan's eyes flared with lust. "It is the mating pull. Come to me now and let me ease you." He lifted her and helped her straddle his lap so her pussy was directly over his cock. He lowered her slowly, pressing the large, mushroomed head to her opening.

"Use your magic to ease her open," Galan said from the opposite side of the bed where he waited, making Brydan snarl at the interference.

Alexis looked over and felt her mouth water as Galan stroked his large cock with his hand. Before she could reach for him, her eyes closed again as she was slowly lowered onto Brydan's cock. The thick crest pushed inside her, parting her muscles and stretching her wide. It felt so wonderful to be filled with him, but she needed more.

She needed it all.

"Oh god, that's good. So good..."

"Slowly, Lexie. Take me slowly, give my magic time to open you for me."

Her hands kneaded the muscles of his chest as he leaned back so he was lying down on the bed, his feet still planted on the floor. His hands were holding her waist and she tried to push herself down on him faster, wanting more of him. A sharp slap on her ass interrupted her pleasure and she turned to glare at Thorn.

"Do not rush it, or else you will hurt yourself on Brydan's cock. You are small, mate, and he does not want to injure you because you are not ready."

"Don't tell me I'm not ready," she growled at him, shocking them all. "I need him. You say you want me, well then show me, damn it!"

"We do want you, more than anything. What is wrong with her?" Thorn shot a worried glance at Xavier who was also at a loss for words.

"She is so tight." Brydan groaned, struggling to remain still. "I am on the brink of losing control already."

"Give her time to—"

"Stop talking about me like I'm not here!" Alexis growled. Choosing to ignore them, she focused on the feeling of Brydan inside her and slammed her hips down on him, impaling herself fully on his shaft. She screamed out as she instantly climaxed as soon as she felt Brydan's cock hit the entrance to her womb. Muscles straining, her pussy clamped down on him so hard she could feel every ridge of his cock.

"Fuck!" Brydan snarled as he felt the muscles of her pussy squeezing his cock so hard he had no choice but to come with her. His seed jetted out, bathing her channel with his release as she grinded against him. His cock swelled, locking him inside her and his body jerked when she rocked her body on him, milking him of every drop of his seed.

Alexis shook as her climax tore through her, but it still wasn't enough. She began jerking her hips against Brydan, seeking to quench the fire in her belly and relished the feeling of his hot release bathing her insides.

Surrounded by the four large, tattooed warriors she should have felt intimidated, apprehensive even, but she didn't. Power surged through her as she basked in the strong emotions pouring off the men in waves. Acute lust battered her system as the rest of the world melted away, leaving the five of them together locked in the passion and the pleasure. Nothing else mattered. She felt like an animal acting on pure instinctual need, and it scared her.

"Oh god, I need more. What's wrong with me?" she cried out.

"I have never seen a female like this before."

"You better not have," Alexis snarled at all of them.

"My love, we wish to mate only you," Thorn assured her.

"Her emotions are out of control. I think she needs the blood bond to center her," Galan said softly, his silver eyes glowing with concern.

"Then we shall claim her now." Xavier gripped her head and leaned forward to take her mouth with his. He drank down her sobs as Brydan began jerking his hips beneath her to prolong her orgasm. The swelling had decreased, but Brydan was still larger than usual so he used shallow jabs until he was able to move more freely. He was still hard even though he just came and she felt him sliding inside her with ease now that her pussy was coated with his release. It felt so good, so right to feel him moving inside her. Reaching out, she tried to grab Xavier's cock with her hand, but he gripped her hand with his instead.

"Do not worry, little one. We will take care of you. Let us give you what you need," Xavier whispered against her lips.

She whimpered as she felt Thorn's fingers against her tight rosebud, and she pushed back against his seeking fingers. "Please, I need…" she whimpered as she tore her mouth away from Xavier's.

"Hush, my love. I will give you what you need, but I need to get you ready," Thorn said as he pushed a finger into her ass, using the copious fluids leaking out from her pussy around Brydan's cock.

The feeling was exquisite. Alexis closed her eyes, enjoying the pleasure of Thorn's finger thrusting into her back hole as she rode Brydan's massive cock.

It was as if her body was no longer her own. She was pure sensation. A living entity whose sole purpose was seeking pleasure from her mates. She felt her body ease open as Thorn added another finger to the first. They stroked and rubbed inside her, stretching her for his possession. Xavier claimed her mouth again, his tongue mating with hers seductively as her other mates pleasured her body. She let out a sound of protest when Thorn pulled his fingers out of her then she shivered as she felt something far thicker pressing against the tiny hole.

"Steady, little one," Xavier whispered, trying to calm her. "Let Thorn in."

She felt the burn as Thorn slowly pushed into her ass and tried to keep her body relaxed. His thick cock slid against his brother's through the thin membrane inside her and it amazed her how easily they both fit inside her. Her fevered mind told her that their magic was doing its thing to allow her to take their massive cocks without pain, and she was extremely grateful for it because something inside of her desperately craved their possession.

"Does it hurt, Alexis?" Thorn asked.

"No," she moaned, enjoying the exquisite feeling of having them both inside her, filling her full. "It's so good. So fucking good. Gimme more."

Doing as she asked, Brydan and Thorn began to thrust, one pulling out as the other surged deeper. She gripped Xavier's hand hard and dug her nails into Brydan's chest with her other hand making him grunt. Galan moved closer to them, helping to hold her up and she gave herself over to them, allowing them to care for her as she simply gave herself over to the ecstasy of been fucked so thoroughly.

She felt Thorn's mouth trailing over her neck, his massive body covering her from behind. It made her shiver as she felt his fangs scrap against the base of her throat. "Yes," she whispered. Brydan sucked on one of her nipples, pleasuring the tight nub with his attention.

They gave her no warning as they both struck at once. Thorn's fangs sank into her neck at the same time Brydan bit into the swell of her breast. She screamed as the feeling of their bites made her come again, harder than the first time.

Thorn growled as Alexis' body squeezed his cock tight like a hot, velvet vise. He wanted to roar out with satisfaction at bringing their mate pleasure as she shuddered between him and his brother. Her blood was like ambrosia, bringing his own desire to the peak as he felt the bond between them snap into place. He was in her mind now, just as she was in his heart. Waves of ecstasy battered at him, making his body tighten as she drove him over the edge with her.

"Pull out," Thorn commanded his brother, even as his own cock swelled within the tight confines of her ass. He let out a roar as hot jets of his semen filled her and Brydan pulled his cock from her pussy, jerking her hips against him hard so that the lips of her sex stroked his cock to climax.

Alexis moaned as they both pulled their heads back after licking the wounds they made. Thorn yanked her back against him, turning her head so his lips could claim hers. The metallic taste of blood filled her mouth and she tried to pull away, but he wouldn't let her. *"Taste me,"* Thorn commanded in her head. *"Bond with me then with Brydan."*

Hearing Thorn in her mind made her realize that he had cut his lip and the blood she was tasting was his. It should have disgusted her, but it didn't. Instead, satisfaction surged through her knowing that she was now blood bonded with him, filling her with a sense of belonging. When he released her she saw Brydan's hand had turned into claws and he'd cut a thin line on his chest, directly over his heart.

"Mate with me, Lexie," Brydan growled.

She could see the plea clear in his glowing golden eyes and pushed aside her aversion to blood to do as he asked. Leaning down she licked at his blood, taking his essence inside her just as he had done. She thought she would have a hard time drinking his blood, but the need to form the bond was strong, almost like a compulsion she couldn't deny.

"You are mine now," Brydan purred in her head and she pulled back to cup his face in her hands.

"And you're mine."

She groaned as Thorn pulled his cock from the tender muscles of her ass. Before she could recover she was lifted off of Brydan and Xavier threw her down on the center of the bed on her back, covering her with his large body.

"You are mine as well," he growled out as he spread her legs with his own, surging into her pussy with one hard thrust, his need for her so great he couldn't wait any longer.

"I am," she promised, holding onto his sweat-slickened arms as he began pounding himself into her. He rose over her like the conquering warrior that he was, muscles straining as he held himself up over her so he didn't crush her into the mattress. Sweat beaded his brow as his hips surged against hers. She met his passion beat for beat, giving herself to him completely. Her head was turned and Galan pressed his cock to her lips.

“I need to feel your mouth on me, sweetling. Take me inside and suckle me.”

Alexis opened for him and reached up to use her hand to stroke his shaft while she swirled her tongue around the head of his cock, reveling at the taste of him. She hummed at the pleasure of feeling his large shaft throbbing in her hand and wanted more. Sucking him deeper, she looked up at him through veiled lashes, watching Galan’s glowing eyes burn brighter as he fed her his cock.

“Good, so good…” Galan groaned as he gently rocked his hips, fucking into her mouth so she didn’t have to move.

Xavier buried his face in her neck on the opposite side where Thorn had bitten her. He needed to bond with her, needed her to give him access into her mind so they could become one. “Your tight little pussy was made for us. You were made for us, mate,” he snarled softly in her ear. “No one else will touch you but us! Say it!”

“I’m yours,” she said breathlessly as she pulled back from Galan’s cock. “And you’re mine!” She quickly went back to sucking Galan into her mouth, using her tongue to lash over the hard nubs underneath the head as Xavier pounded her into the bed.

“Mine!”

Alexis moaned in response, loving how possessive they all were of her. Something about the way Xavier snarled the word made her feel cherished beyond anything she’d ever known. They were all she needed and she was overjoyed that all four males were bound to her.

Her back arched off the bed and she cried out, pulling off of Galan’s cock completely as Xavier’s fangs sank into her neck. Lost in a sea of sensation, Alexis felt Xavier merge with her, into her mind and heart just as Thorn and Brydan had. Her body shattered as she came again, the pleasure bordered on pain it was so intense.

Desperate pleas fell from her lips and her body bucked beneath him. She didn’t know if she was trying to fight the sheer bliss he was forcing on her or trying to get closer. Either way, she had no control and had to trust that they wouldn't let her fall to pieces.

"Never, mate. We will always be here to catch you," Thorn promised from where he was sitting by her side.

Xavier felt her emotions through the bond he created with her and it made him crazy to feel how much she wanted him. The agonizing ache inside of him eased now that she was finally his and he pulled back, needing to complete the bond with her. Transforming his own hand into a claw, he cut a thin line over his heart so she could drink from him.

"Drink from me, little one. Drink and complete the mating bond."

Lifting her head to him, Xavier growled at the pleasure of feeling her take his essence into her. He felt the blood bond snap in place and pistoned his hips faster against her, slamming his cock into her hard and fast.

Alexis cried out his name as she came again, not even coming down from her first one and Xavier let himself follow her over the edge. He thrust once, twice more, then felt his cock explode, filling her depths with his seed as his cock swelled inside her.

Galan fisted his cock in his hand, squeezing tight to stave off the need to come as he watched their mate writhing under his brother's body. By the Gods, she was so beautiful it was hard to believe that she truly belonged to them now. She was glorious to watch as she cried out in ecstasy, and he couldn't wait to be the one to bring her such pleasure himself. As soon as Xavier was able to pull back, Galan took his place. Pushing his cock into her dripping pussy, he growled as he felt her muscles rippling around him.

"Mate with me, sweetling."

"With pleasure, Galan."

Her dreamy smile made him feel like a god, and he saw the happiness in her beautiful violet eyes as she stared up at him. He began moving inside her slowly at first, waiting for her to come down from her release before he sent her over the edge again. She wrapped her long legs around his waist as he fucked his cock in and out of her, and he watched those violet eyes haze over with the pleasure he gave her.

Control ravaged, he fought to keep his pace steady. He needed to give her this, to give her everything. Since the first time he had taken her he had known she belonged to them and cursed himself for not recognizing the signs of the mating before she had been hurt during the dinner. He hated knowing that she had been uncertain about their commitment to her for even one minute, and now he would make sure there was no doubt that she belonged to them.

When he was close to coming, Galan lowered his head and sank his fangs into the swell of her breast, directly over her heart, and drank down the sweet taste of her blood to bond her to him. He felt her tighten around him and heard her cry out his name as her body bucked beneath his, drawing him impossibly deeper.

After licking the wound closed, he bite down hard on his lower lip then pressed them against hers, needing her to take him inside her so they were one. She opened for him immediately and he felt their minds merge through their blood bond. Feeling her pleasure through their bond he came, his cock swelling as he pumped his hot seed into her body, claiming her as his mate.

It was done.

Alexis was their mate.

She belonged to them now, and no one would ever take her from them and they would kill anyone who was foolish enough to try. He felt her body go lax beneath him and he pulled back to see the fatigue stealing her away.

“Thank you for giving yourself to us, Alexis.”

“It was my pleasure.” She smiled dreamily at him as she panted for breath. “Give me a few minutes then we can go for round two.”

Galan chuckled as he rubbed his nose against her cheek. He breathed deep, loving the scent of her skin. He could sense the changes beginning within her and knew she would need healing sleep to help her complete the conversion her body needed to go through to make her like them.

Alexis looked around at the three men sitting on the side of the bed then back up at Galan who was still braced over her and laughed.

"What is so funny, mate?" Thorn asked, reaching out to stroke his hand over her hair.

"Jesus, you guys are huge. I think we need a bigger bed. I think we broke this one, or is the room tilting?"

The males all chuckled. "Aye, we did break it," Galan agreed. "The bed was not meant to hold our combined weight."

"This will be so much fun to explain to the cleaning crew." Alexis groaned as Galan slowly pulled his cock out of her, shifting off of her. Sprawled out in front of all four of her mates should have made her feel self-conscious, but she didn't have the energy to worry about that. Hell, she didn't even have the energy to move at all.

"Rest easy, mate. Let us care for you."

Ah, the blood bond thing. Alexis could feel all four males inside her head…and in her heart. They belonged to her now.

"Aye, we are yours. Forever," Xavier vowed. "As you belong to us."

With that thought, she closed her eyes and drifted off with a smile on her face.

Chapter Seven

"What the fuck?"

Alexis jackknifed up in bed, slamming her hands over her ears as she woke with a start. She could hear her own heart beating like a damn drum in her head, not to mention the various sounds coming from outside sounded like they were coming from right inside the bedroom.

Thorn gently eased her back down onto the bed, rubbing at her bare arms in comfort. "Rest easy, mate. Your senses are heightened now. Just imagine turned down a dial in your mind, and it will go back to normal."

She closed her eyes and focused on turning down the volume in her head and was surprised when it actually worked. When she opened her eyes again she saw that it was daylight and both Thorn and Xavier were looking down at her with amusement flashing in their glowing eyes.

Her own eyes narrowed in response. "You think this is funny?"

"Aye, mate, and a good rising to you as well," Xavier said as he leaned down to brush his lips against hers.

When he tried to push into her with his tongue she resisted. "Morning breath," she muttered, trying to keep her lips sealed. He chuckled then her eyes widened as the clean taste of mint flooded her mouth. "Oh, wow."

"You have only to ask and we will provide, mate," Xavier murmured before he sealed his mouth over hers, his tongue delving deep.

"I think I can really get used to you and your magic. Talk about convenience in a rock hard package!" she said with a wink. Xavier chuckled then growled as her hand trailed down to stroke over his erection, gripping him.

"We cannot linger," Thorn said from his side of the bed, his voice filled with regret. "Galan and Brydan are already anxiously waiting."

Xavier let out a deep sigh. "Aye, I know. How do you feel this rising, little one?"

As both males watched her, Alexis stretched on the bed like a contented feline, making them groan as their cocks swelled. "I feel great. What?" she asked as they continued to eye her as if they were waiting for something. "What's wrong?"

"You feel no different?" Xavier asked carefully.

Alexis paused as she took mental stock of herself. She figured after taking all four of them last night she would have woken up sore as hell. Their cocks were massive and she was so much smaller than them, but she didn't feel the slightest amount of discomfort now. In fact, she felt wonderful, better than she had ever felt before. She was mated to four gorgeous Dragon Warriors now and she was now…

Oh, holy shit!

She stilled. "Galan said something about a conversion last night. Am I like you now?"

"Aye, you are," Thorn confirmed. "We thought it best to put you in a healing sleep while your body went through the changes."

She gaped at them. "What changes exactly?"

Thorn and Xavier glanced at each other and she knew they were speaking to each other through their own bond. She could feel the energy hum over her skin like a small power surge. Reaching out, she yanked hard one of the small braids they both wore on the sides of their temples.

"Alexis!" Thorn gasped as Xavier growled in pain.

"Stop talking to each other and answer me! I can feel you talking and it's making me uncomfortable."

That got their immediate attention. "What do you mean by uncomfortable?"

“I feel it,” she huffed out. She could feel both of them weren’t satisfied with her answer then felt both of them linking to her through their blood bonds. Damn, she was going to have to get used to them being in her head now.

Talk about a serious lack of personal space!

Thorn leaned in and kissed her lightly as if in apology. “You will become accustomed to it. Being merged with us will become as natural as breathing.”

“I don’t think so,” she muttered. She was a woman with four very powerful, very pushy mates. There was no way she was ever going to feel comfortable with them popping in and out of her head.

Xavier sighed. “You will have privacy if you wish it, but we need to know what you are feeling to best care for you.”

“You could always just ask me, you know,” she grumbled, still not convinced.

“Aye, we could, but you must also answer us,” Xavier countered. “We were not aware that your gifts of empathy would make you sensitive enough to feel us speaking through our bond and needed to know exactly what it was doing to you to ensure you were not in pain.”

Fair enough, he had a point. “It wasn’t pain, I could just sense you were speaking.”

“Aye, we sensed what you felt,” Thorn said with a nod. “We have converted you and you are now like us. The change has healed your body fully and you will be able to adjust all of your senses at your will. Lights will no longer bother you so there will be no need for your eye coverings when we are outdoors.”

Xavier placed his hand over her stomach. “You are also healed here.”

She placed her hand over his, holding it to her as she closed her eyes. Joy filled her and her eyes flooded with tears as she took a moment to fully appreciate the gift she had been given. Xavier and

Thorn cuddled close to her so she was surrounded by both of them and they kissed away the tears that leaked out of her eyes.

"Do not weep, my love," Thorn whispered. "As we said, you have only to ask and we will provide."

Alexis opened her eyes and stared up at him with all the love she was feeling. And she did love these males. Somehow, she had fallen in love with Thorn, Xavier, Galan and Brydan, and she was so damn happy that they were mated. She finally belonged somewhere, after being alone for so long.

"You will never be alone again," Xavier said softly.

"Thank you," she whispered as she caressed Xavier's cheek before she pressed her lips to his. When she was done she turned her head and did the same to Thorn.

"Your pleasure is ours," Xavier said solemnly. Alexis wanted to kiss him again, but a voice in her head stopped her.

"Our mate wants to shower in the ways of her people," Brydan said in their heads, interrupting the moment. *"If you do not take her into the shower right now, Galan and I would be more than happy to do so. Our meal is almost prepared and we will not wait much longer to see our mate."*

"He is, how would you say it? Not a morning person," Thorn said dryly.

Alexis laughed as she sat up in bed. She realized that her body was completely clean and sometime during the night they had also fixed the bed they had broken. Their magic really was kick-ass, but she still did want to take a shower. Even if it wasn't necessary, it was one of those morning rituals that she enjoyed and didn't want to stop.

"Then we shall shower with you," Xavier offered as he lifted her from the bed easily, carrying her into the bathroom.

Alexis tapped him on the shoulder, wanting to be put down as soon as they were inside the large bathroom. "Why don't you start the shower while I take care of…" She pointed toward the small separate room that housed the toilet. Both Thorn and Xavier smirked at her.

"We are your mates, there is nothing you should hide from us."

"This is so not something we are going to be discussing. Ever. Now, go," she ordered, shooing them away with a wave of her hand as she closed the door behind her. She waited until she heard the sound of running water before she took care of her business and flushed. When she came out, Thorn walked in after her, not closing the door while he took care of his morning needs. She hurried away and rolled her eyes as she heard him laughing at her.

She absently glanced at herself in the mirror as she passed by it on her way to the shower and stopped dead in her tracks.

What the hell?

Gaping at herself in shock she barely noticed that Thorn was walking up behind her as Xavier took his place in the small adjacent room. She didn't say anything as she continued to stare at herself in the mirror, blinking in disbelief.

"You are…distressed," Thorn finally said as Xavier came to stand beside him.

"You think?" she growled out.

What the hell did they think? That she would just be okay the first time she saw that her eyes were freaking glowing? Her eyes had already been an unusual bright violet color, but now? Hell, they were glowing violet, like two fucking purple stars…just like theirs.

"This—" she growled, pointing to her eyes "—is what you should have said when I asked you about what freaking changes were made to my body. We really need to work on your communications skill, because they obviously suck!"

She stomped away from the mirror and entered the large shower enclosure, letting the hot water soothe her irritation. Apparently all males, human or not, had the spectacular ability to piss women off. She hadn't really thought about all the changes that would happen to her when she allowed them to change her and she didn't regret it. Still, it was going to take some getting used to and it would have helped if they warned her before her eyes started glowing or her hearing went all wacky.

What else could she look forward to discovering about herself?

Alexis felt Thorn and Xavier enter behind her and was able to ignore them until she felt their large hands stroking over her skin. Opening one eye under the spray, she looked at their somber faces.

"Forgive us, mate. We did not realize it would upset you so," Thorn said.

She sighed. Of course they wouldn't think there was anything wrong since they were so used to being what they were. She couldn't seem to hold onto her annoyance with them stroking body-wash all over her. She gave into the pleasure as she stood under the gentle spray of water, allowing them to care for her.

Thorn stood behind her, rubbing shampoo in her hair and his fascination with the bubbles made her want to giggle. They informed her that on their ship they had water from their homeworld that both cleansed and healed them so they had no need for shampoo or soap. Xavier took his time massaging her breasts until they were full and aching, her nipples tight peaks that poked into the center of his large palms. She knew they didn't have time for another round of love play in the shower, but she wanted to touch them, to fill the need she had to explore their perfect bodies.

She grabbed the bottle of body-wash and poured some of the creamy liquid into the palm of her hand, eyeing Xavier's gorgeous body as he knelt in front of her, cleaning her legs and feet with long, sure strokes. She still couldn't believe these males were truly hers. Xavier was like some mythical god, all hard muscles under golden skin. The dark lines of their tattoos made her hands ache to touch them. She wanted to run her hands all over their strong bodies, and even better, trace those lines with her tongue.

She smiled to herself. There would be time for that. They belonged to her now and she'd have plenty of time to explore their bodies to her heart's content. She didn't just have one perfect male, she had four.

Damn, she was a lucky girl.

"I think I've figured it out."

Xavier stood at her statement and cocked his head in question. Giving into her need, she reach out and stroked her hand over Xavier's thick cock, making him freeze.

"What have you figured out, my love?"

Alexis smiled at Thorn's nickname for her and squeezed tighter on Xavier's shaft, making him groan. She found she was fascinated by their large cocks and loved to touch them whenever she could. She could spend hours stroking them with her hands, sucking them, or even just feeling them pressed against her skin so she could feel them pulsing to the rhythm of their hearts. But most of all, she loved feeling them inside her, sliding deep in her pussy or ass until they spurted their hot seed inside her.

"I cannot concentrate while you are playing with my cock, mate," Xavier growled. "And those thoughts are going to get you fucked again then Galan and Brydan will kill us for making them wait longer."

Alexis laughed as she leaned back, letting Thorn wash the shampoo out of her hair. Damn, she couldn't seem to remember the whole mind meld thing. It was strange how comfortable she felt with both of them standing in the shower naked. But then again, she had a feeling she was going to have to get used to them pretty damn quick with four extremely large, very alpha males slipping in and out of her head.

Having them in her mind was more intimate than anything she had ever experienced before, and she didn't think she could describe it to someone even if she tried. It was like becoming a part of someone else, and sharing herself with all four of them got easier with every passing minute despite her reservations.

Even if it was weird having them in her head, she loved having access to their minds. The blood bond thing sure helped with trying to figure out the complexities of deciphering the male psyche.

Feeling Xavier's pleasure, she continued to move her hand over his cock with slow, steady stroked then shifted to grab Thorn's with her other hand. His hands stilled in the process of rubbing the conditioner into her hair. Looking at both of them, she rubbed her thumbs over the ridges under the head of their cocks enjoying their reactions to her touch. She tilted her head back, allowing the water to wash the cream out of her hair and smiled as they both groaned when her breasts jutted out from her stance.

"What was I saying? Oh yes, I think I figured out the whole mating thing without the blood bond," she said, watching how their eyes glowed with unbridled lust. For her. It was all for her and she could not only sense it with her empathic powers, but she could also feel it through their bond. Every stroke over their shafts brought waves of pleasure to them, and in turn, feeling their emotions stroked her own fire curling in her belly.

"I think the bond your race creates—"

"Your race as well," Thorn corrected her. "You are one of us now."

"Yes, I am, aren't I?" She smiled at them. "I think the bond you created with me started when you came inside me that first time. When I had sex with you and Galan—"

Xavier growled. "We made love to our mate."

She rolled her eyes. "I wasn't your mate yet. But you made me so when you filled me with your cum."

"Aye, we filled you," Xavier growled, his glowing silver eyes burning even brighter as he remembered back to that first time he took her. He was having trouble thinking as their mate stroked his straining flesh. He was delighted at the pleasure she took from touching him and Thorn, and he would always welcome her hands on him. Feeling the enjoyment she took from having her hand on him had a rush sweeping through him that brought him closer to the point of climax.

He had underestimated her talent as an empath, and he didn't know if she understood how that power had grown when they had converted her. Instead of simply absorbing the emotions coming from him and Thorn, she was merging those feelings with her own and sending them back to them through their bond tenfold.

"We have never released our seed into any other female we have taken over these long years before you," Thorn explained, his thought clouded with the need for release. He sucked his breath in harshly as Alexis' grip tightened on him.

"It's bad form to speak of sleeping with another woman when I have my hands on your junk," she growled viciously at Thorn, making him wince.

"I did not mean it like that, my love."

Logic told her it was true, but she didn't care. She was determined to make it so they couldn't even think about another woman while they were with her. She stroked them harder, moving up and down their thick shafts with ruthless determination. "Your pleasure belongs to me now," she snarled.

"Aye, mate," Xavier growled back.

"It does," Thorn swore.

Primal need filled her now. She wanted, needed to show them that they were hers just as she belonged to them. In a shocking display of possession, she worked her hands back and forth faster until she coaxed their climax from them so their hot seed shot onto her stomach, coating her with their essence. They growled in unison as their cocks swelled and both Xavier and Thorn palmed their own shafts around hers, helping to milk every drop from them as they let her control their pleasure.

Emotions converged inside her and she felt overloaded. Stars burst behind her eyes as she felt her own orgasm rock her body, her clit pulsing with each spurt of their cum so they came together in glorious release. The pearly liquid ran down her body, mixing with the water pouring over her as shame struck. She pulled her hands away, but before she could turn from them Xavier took her mouth in a brutal kiss.

"You have nothing to feel shame for, little one. Our pleasure does belong to you and I have no issue with you showing us whenever you wish," Xavier said through their bond.

She pulled away and leaned her head on his broad chest. "I know, but I shouldn't have done it like that…in anger. I don't know what's wrong with me. I keep acting like a bitch and I can't seem to control it."

Thorn gently pulled her from Xavier's arms and wrapped her in his strong embrace. "Your emotions are heightened by your empathic powers. I should have never mentioned other females when we were sharing time together like this. We would have reacted the same way if you had mentioned being with other males."

As a growl tore from Xavier, Thorn raised a brow. "See what I mean?"

Alexis laughed as she wrapped her arms around Thorn's waist, needing his warmth. Xavier turned off the water and Thorn lifted her, carrying her from the shower. They dried her slowly, enjoying the simple task as they explained how her empathic abilities would be difficult to handle until she relearned how to control them again.

"I just don't understand why I got so mad," she said with a huff of breath.

"Your dragon spirit is part of you now. Your animal side will not allow any to come between you and your mates," Xavier said easily.

Oh, for the love of...

"Is this something else you forgot to mention? Dragon spirit?"

"Aye, my love. As we are Dragon Warriors, you now also possess the ability to shift into your dragon form," Thorn explained.

"This is also information I could have used earlier!" Alexis tried slapped her palm against her forehead, only Xavier caught her arm before she could make contact.

"Do not strike yourself!" he growled down at her.

"I wasn't going to hurt myself," she growled back, jerking her arm from him then she threw both of her hands in the air. "And I just realized I'm growling now, too! You guys really suck at sharing information!"

Xavier suddenly laughed. "You are a delight to me, mate. As we have never mated before, there is much to learn…for all of us."

She smiled. "I guess you're right."

They got dressed and walked into the living room of the suite where Galan and Brydan were sitting waiting for her. She loved how she immediately had all her mates attention as if they couldn't wait to see her.

"It is because we cannot," Galan said as he rose from his seat to kiss her.

Shit, she would have to remember that mind reading thing now.

Galan chuckled against her lips then she was pulled away and swept up into Brydan's embrace. He growled as his mouth crushed down on hers and she opened for him immediately, allowing his tongue to delve deep.

"I have not come in my pants since I was a youngling," Brydan growled as he set her back on her feet.

"You…what?" Her eyes widened as her gaze dropped down to look at the bulge in his pants. All four of the males had dressed in their standard black leather pants and she could see that Brydan's impressive erection was still swollen within the confines of his pants.

"Aye, I am still hard and aching for you, Lexie. And you will soon see to it for real and not just with your mind next time," Brydan said.

Galan took possession of her again and sat down at the table with her in his lap. “Your bond with us is strong, sweetling. When you were pleasuring our brothers our minds were connected and you fed us your passion so it felt as if you were stroking us as well.”

“Oh wow,” Alexis breathed out. Obviously, Thorn and Xavier were right about her powers being out of control. She would have to relearn how to control her gifts, but how cool was it that she could make her mates come in another room simply from sharing her own pleasure with them? It was amazing. But making Brydan and Galan come in their pants…she should feel bad about that, shouldn’t she?

Galan leaned down and nipped at her ear with his teeth making her shudder. “You seem to enjoy the power you have over us, mate. Perhaps we need to show you how we control your pleasure as well.”

Alexis’ desire to have Galan show her exactly what he was talking about was halted as Thorn, Brydan and Xavier sat down at the table with them. “Nay, not yet. Our mate needs to eat and then we need to start our journey,” Thorn warned.

Brydan growled with impatience then settle himself as he leaned forward to pick up a strawberry and held it to her lips. She took his offering and moaned as the fresh flavor burst over her taste buds. Suddenly realizing how hungry she was, she looked at the platters of food covering the table with greedy eyes.

“You did not eat last night and we worked you hard last eve,” Galan said as he lifted a piece of roasted chicken to her lips.

“You need to eat more,” Brydan agreed.

Alexis felt herself blush at his reference as she chewed. “I didn’t realize how hungry I was until I saw all this food. This isn’t exactly breakfast fare though.”

“I believe we ordered enough,” Galan said with a gleam of amusement in his eyes. “We need to keep up our strength now that we have a mate to please.”

Brydan and Galan had laid out a feast while she had been busy with Thorn and Xavier in the shower. The Alliance had made sure to house several restaurants in the lower levels of the building that provided delivery service to any visitors staying in the suites. The food provided by the establishments were top-quality, and there was a wide selection that would cater to an assortment of tastes of the visiting aliens.

From the mass amount of food laid out on the table, Galan and Brydan had apparently ordered something from each of the restaurants. There were large platters of several different types of meats, freshly baked bread, cheese and other delicacies on the table. Off to the side there was even a tray of flaky pastries that looked so good they made Alexis' mouth water.

She watched with sheer amazement as Xavier, Thorn, Galan and Brydan began to devour the food, with Brydan and Galan taking turns feeding her. It felt decadent to have her mates feed her, but she simply let herself enjoy the meal being provided for her and consumed enough to sate her hunger. When she told them she was full all four males frowned at her then proceeded to finish off the rest of the food.

While they ate, her mates had told her about all the exotic planets they had visited over their long years of travel. They spoke of far off worlds where only animals roamed. They told her of a planet where female warriors ruled and they'd had to escape from being captured as breeders by using their magic. There were planets where hostile enemies laid in wait, wanting nothing to do with visitors. There were also various worlds of shifters, of other magical beings that didn't travel the stars yet. It still amazed her that she would be able to see those locations with her own eyes soon. Thinking about that reminded her of something Thorn said earlier.

"Thorn?"

Immediately she had his full attention. "Aye, my love?"

"You mentioned a journey earlier. Were you, or I should say, are we going to be leaving Earth soon?"

Thorn smiled at her. "Nay, mate. We will stay here long enough for you to settle what you need before we leave. I was speaking of our need to journey to open land soon."

"We need to let our dragons free," Xavier added. "We always take the opportunity when we are on a planet's surface to roam the land in our dragon forms since we cannot do so on board our ship."

Alexis' eyes brightened with interest. She couldn't wait to see them in their dragon forms. "There is a place I would love to take you guys. It's called Crystal Cove. There is a large clearing and a waterfall. I've only been there a few times when I patrolled the area when I was still in the Academy. It's absolutely beautiful, but it's near the border of the badlands so it could be dangerous."

Brydan snorted at that then his eyes narrowed. "Do you honestly think we would ever let any harm come to you?"

Through their bond she could feel that she had offended all of them with her warning. That wasn't her intention at all. Warning them of the dangers had simply been her first reaction at the thought of venturing so close to the badlands. The Alliance didn't have a stronghold in certain areas outside of the major cities and it was more difficult to regulate what went on there. Due to that, the badlands were a haven for rebels and others who didn't believe in living by Alliance rules and regulations. Alexis relaxed in Galan's arms, known full well that her four mates would never let anything happen to her. She smiled. "Of course not. I apologize for even suggesting such a thing."

"You find this amusing, mate?" Xavier growled, even as his eyes glowed bright with amusement.

"I don't know what you are talking about," she teased. "Let me call into my commander and have him clear a flight path for us. I wouldn't want any soldiers taking shots at us when they see us flying overhead."

After Galan reluctantly released her, she got up and went to grab her wrist unit from the bedroom where she'd left it. "I can't wait to ride a dragon through the skies," she called out over her shoulder with a laugh.

"We would be happy to have you ride one of us, mate," Thorn said. "But why would you want to do that when you could fly yourself?"

She stumbled over her own feet as she spun around to gape at them. Well, hell, she had completely forgotten about that part of the change. Alexis couldn't imagine being able to shape-shift into another form, and the mere thought was both exhilarating and terrifying. "Umm, yeah. Forget I said that."

Inside the bedroom she found that one of her mates had picked up her dress and wrist unit where they had been left on the floor. The dress now lay draped over a chair and the write unit had been carefully placed on her dresser. It made her smile to see how they had taken care of her things when she had been beyond thinking about it last night when they had taken her to bed.

Attaching the wrist unit she logged in and brought up the screen to place a call then hesitated. Remembering that she now had glowing eyes, she ordered, "Video off. Contact Commander Spartan, audio only."

"Spartan."

"Commander—" she said as soon as he answered and wasn't surprised when he cut her off.

"What the hell happened last night, Lex? And why the fuck is your video off? Are you in trouble? Is something wrong?"

She couldn't help but smile as he barked out his questions and knew the harsh rasp of his voice was only because he was worried about her. Once you were under Jax Spartan's protection he took it very seriously. "I'm fine, Jax."

"I do not like the way he is speaking to you," Xavier growled from the doorway.

Alexis held back the urge to roll her eyes and raise a finger up to her lips asking for him to remain quiet then beckoned him into the room with her. Xavier sat down on the bed and pulled her onto his lap, holding her close. She curled into him, allowing her head to fall onto his shoulder as he stroked a hand over her back. *"Jax doesn't mean anything by it,"* she assured Xavier through their bond. *"He is like a brother to me and is only worried. He doesn't know you and wants to make sure I'm okay."*

"Then tell him you now belong to us and we shall care for you instead. He has no need to worry about you any longer," Xavier arrogantly replied.

This time Alexis did roll her eyes then switched her focus back to the call as Jax let out his own frustrated growl.

"They're there with you now? Lex, if you don't answer me I swear I am going to—"

"Do not raise your voice to my mate," Xavier warned, his voice a deadly growl.

There was silence over the line then Jax finally spoke. "Lex? Could you explain what he means by that? You're his mate?"

"Umm, yeah. Sorry, Jax. Obviously, I have a lot to tell you," Alexis said, deliberately using his first name to make the call more informal. "Xavier is with me right now. The others are in another room. Things have been…there is so much to explain, I don't really know where to begin…"

Because he was her friend as well as her commander, Alexis explained everything to Jax, only leaving out the more intimate details of what had happened between her and the Dragon Warriors. When she was done she waited patiently for Jax's response as Xavier brushed his lips over her forehead, enjoying the feeling of him running his fingers through her long hair.

"Holy fucking shit," Jax finally said when she was done.

"Yeah, tell me about it," Alexis replied with a laugh.

"This is…hell, I'm speechless," Jax admitted. "Is this what you really want?"

Xavier let out a growl, but Alexis pressed her lips to his to silence him. When she pulled back she made sure to stare into his eyes as she answered Jax, letting Xavier see the truth in what she said.

"Trust me, this wasn't expected, but this is right for me. I know it's crazy since I just met them, but they are a part of me now, just as I'm a part of them. They are my future, Jax. I've finally found where I belong."

"I'm happy for you, Lex," Jax said then he sighed. "This is going to be…complicated to explain, but I'm behind you all the way. Just remember, magic or no magic, those Dragon Warriors better treat you right. Archer and I will kick their asses if they hurt you. I don't know how, but we'll find a way."

"Commander Spartan," Xavier said, breaking into the conversation. "Since my mate claims you as a brother, I will tell you that Alexis owns our hearts and souls. Hurting her would be like hurting ourselves. It is our duty to care for her and place her happiness above our own."

Alexis' heart melted as she felt the love flowing from Xavier. How could she not love a man who said stuff like that?

"Well," Jax breathed out. "I guess I can't ask for anything more."

"But know this, we will not allow anyone to come between our mating…even you," Xavier said forcefully. "We would challenge your entire world to keep her with us."

"I'm sure it won't ever come to that." Jax chuckled. "Lex, you seem to be in good hands."

"I really am," she agreed, blushing as she remembered just how good her mates were with their hands. "I know it's a lot to take in, but I really am happy, Jax. You'll see how great we are together, but we have to go now. Speaking of, I actually need you to do mc a favor. Well, it's an official request really."

"Name it."

"They want to see some of the land so I'm going to take them out to the border, over near the Crystal Cove."

"Are you sure that's a good idea? That's pretty damn close to the badlands."

Alexis laughed. "As I was reminded by my mates when I mentioned that, they do have magic and they are warriors in their own right. I can't imagine any of the rebels will want to mess with them."

"True," Jax said with a laugh. "You can take them there, but you have to be back by this weekend in time for the celebration. The regents won't be happy if you miss it and besides, if I have to dress the hell up, you better be there."

"I'll make sure we attend. Don't worry."

"Good. I can clear a transpo for you there at the visitors center and—"

"That won't be necessary," Alexis broke in. "Just clear a flight path from here to the Crystal Cove for us and we'll see you in a few days. Oh, and can you make sure to tell the patrols not to shoot at the dragons in the sky? That would just piss us off. Thanks, Jax!"

"Dragons?" Jax asked incredulously.

Alexis cut off the call and had to laugh. That should give her commander something to think about.

"You are trouble, mate," Xavier said playfully as he cupped her face, tilting it up for his kiss. "I think we will have our hands full with you."

"You can count on it," Alexis promised then she grinned. "Come on and teach me how to fly!"

"Well, here we are..."

Standing on the roof of the visiting center high above the city, Alexis was damn glad that heights didn't bother her.

She tilted her face up to the sun, breathing in the clean air. The colors she was seeing were incredible and it felt like she was viewing everything for the first time. Bright and beautiful, it was amazing being able to stand out in the sunlight without it hurting her eyes. Thankfully, Jax had cleared the landing pad of other soldiers so they didn't have an audience as she stood out there with her four mates. Looking out over the Capital gave her a deep sense of pride at what they had accomplished over the years.

The view truly was spectacular.

"You are the one who is spectacular, mate," Brydan growled as he wrapped his arms around her waist, pulling her back against him.

She sighed in contentment as she snuggled back against him. "I'm glad you think so."

"We know it is so," Thorn said with conviction, making her smile.

Xavier stood with his hands braced on his hips as he looked out over the city. "What your people have accomplished since we were last here is impressive. Humans are a resilient race."

"We are," she agreed.

Xavier turned, his piercing silver eyes serious. "You are no longer human, mate."

Shit, she'd forgotten about that already.

She sent him a sheepish smile. "Right. So how do I go about becoming a dragon?"

"I will show you. Keep your mind open to mine as I bring forth the change and follow how I do it," Thorn told her as he stepped away from the group.

She felt the rush of power surge through Thorn as she focused on him through their bond. She could feel him calling his dragon spirit to him and felt the change happen as he allowed the magic flowing through him to alter his form.

One second, Thorn was a man…the next a large dragon stood in his place.

Alexis' mouth dropped open in awe as she looked up at the magnificent beast standing before her. The dragon's body was covered with iridescent scales that shimmered in the sunlight. It seemed to glow a pearly light-gold to a sparkling deep-bronze, the color changing as its massive chest billowed out as it breathed. Lethal-sharp talons tapped against the ground as he took a step toward her. Those claws looked terrifying, and yet she knew they would never harm her. A large, spiked tail swished back and forth over the ground as enormous wings expanded, stirring the wind so it blew softly against her skin.

She had seen vids before, but nothing compared to seeing a dragon in real life. The dragon was huge, towering over her, but she could see the intelligence shining back at her through those golden eyes. They were Thorn's eyes and she could see the love shining back at her through them as he patiently waited for her reaction.

Alexis pulled away from Brydan slowly, walking over to Thorn. Excitement had her body vibrating as she approached and adrenaline rushed through her as she held out her hand. The dragon lowered its majestic head and gently pushed its nose against her palm.

"Oh my god…" she breathed out. "You are amazing."

"I am pleased you think so."

She ran her hand over his nose then walked around him, stroking her hand over his side. He was a powerful beast with hard scales that protected his body like a coat of armor, yet he trembled beneath her hand as she touched him.

Startled, her eyes raised to his. "Can you feel that?"

"Aye, my love. I have never let another touch my dragon form and it feels amazing."

"I'm glad you've never let someone else touch you. It makes this even more special for me." She walked back to his head so she could look back into his eyes. "Can I really change into a dragon too? It seems too fantastical to imagine."

"You can feel your own dragon spirit within your soul. You have our magic in you now. Feel it humming beneath your skin. Call forth the change, mate, and fly the skies with me," Thorn said though their bond.

"Come join us, little one," Xavier commanded.

Alexis turned her head and saw another large dragon behind her. This one was covered with large iridescent scales that shimmered silver to a glittering dark-gray, and she knew it was Xavier.

Centering herself, she closed her eyes and focused on doing as they asked. She could feel her mates feeding her their strength, encouraging her to call forth the dragon spirit that seemed to be waiting inside her for this very purpose. Stars bursts behind her eyelids, and a wrenching pain struck her body as the change began. "It hurts," she whimpered through gritted teeth.

"Relax, sweetling," Galan said softly. "You are fighting the change. Give yourself over to it and become one with your dragon. It is already inside of you. All you have to do is trust yourself and the dragon spirit."

"We would never let anything hurt you," Brydan added. "No fear, mate."

No fear…

Repeating that mantra in her head, she forced herself to let go. Pure white light engulfed her as she embraced the magic within her until she felt one with an ancient power so potent it was like becoming one with the universe. She let it spread through her, filling every fiber of her being until she felt the dragon spirit merge with her so they became one.

The spirit of the dragon was neither male nor female. It was simply an untapped source of energy that flooded her mind with knowledge of the ages and such strength it stole her breath, making her feel utterly invincible. Her senses were in overdrive, allowing her to feel as if she had somehow connected to the very Earth itself.

The light faded and she opened her eyes, looking out at the world through the eyes of her dragon. Her large head moved fluidly to look over at Galan and Brydan to see them looking back at her with pride glowing in their eyes. Everything became clear to her in that one blinding moment. She was no longer Alexis Donovan, an infertile female. She wasn't even a liaison officer for the United Federation Command Alliance.

She was Alexis, the true mate to Xavier, Galan, Thorn and Brydan, and a Dragon Warrior.

Brydan smiled as he watched their mate flap her wings. She was glorious. Her dragon form was something he had never seen before, shimmering from a pearly-white to silver then to a pale gold color. Using their magic, an individual's dragon usually took on the color that best represented them. It warmed his heart to see that Alexis' dragon form had taken on a little of all of her mates, showing how deeply engrained they were in her heart. Her beautiful violet eyes glowed brightly within the dragon's face as looked at all of them, sharing her joy.

He endeavored never to do anything that would breach that trust or love she felt for them. Alexis was vital to all of them. Without her, the world would no longer hold any meaning. All the long, lonely years they had waited were worth it in order to have her with them now. Rage filled him at the thought of anything happening to her, but he calmed as he watched her spread her wings and her laughter filled his mind.

"This is unbelievable!" she called out.

"You are a natural, Lexie," Brydan said, aware that he was grinning like a fool as her happiness became infectious.

"Come, mate. Take us to this special place of yours," Xavier beckoned. He and Thorn launched themselves into the sky, hovering in place as they waited for Alexis to follow them.

"Okay," Alexis said hesitantly. *"Here goes nothing..."*

Brydan watched as Alexis flapped her wings, building up momentum before she leaped up into the air, hovering effortlessly.

"I did it!"

"Aye, you did," Thorn said. *"We are so proud of you, mate."*

Her laughter rained down on him as he used their bond to monitor her thoughts to ensure she wasn't afraid. He felt no fear inside of her, only exhilaration and pleasure. Alexis had fully merged with her dragon spirit and her dragon would allow no harm to come to her.

Even though all the males could sense Alexis had embraced her dragon, Galan changed into his dragon form and took to the skies as soon as she lifted off, staying slightly below her in case she faltered on her first flight. His protective nature allowing nothing else. They watched as Alexis' smaller dragon flew around each of the males, and they laughed at her antics.

"This is so cool! I can't believe I'm really a dragon!"

Alexis looked down at Brydan and if a dragon could smile, she clearly was. *"Come on, Brydan!"*

A sound had Brydan turning and he saw four soldiers walk out onto the rooftop watching the dragons in shock. His eyes narrowed, watching the soldiers for any sign of hostility, but the soldiers made no move towards them. They simply stood in place by the doorway, watching the dragons with awed expressions.

Satisfied that his family wasn't in jeopardy, Brydan shot them a grin as he altered forms and launched himself into the sky, letting out a triumphant bellow as he followed the other dragons as they flew away from the city that lay spread out beneath them.

Chapter Eight

They landed in a clearing not far from the waterfall, and Alexis shifted back to human form as soon as her feet touched the ground. Looking down at herself, she was amazed that she was still wearing the clothing she had put on before they'd left the suite.

"You were not paying attention, mate," Xavier said as he strode over to pull her into his arms. "I clothed you when you changed back. You must remember to use your magic when you shift. All you have to do is think about what you want to wear and will it. I would not like for anyone else to see your naked form."

She rolled her eyes at him. "It's not like I want to go prancing naked in front of strangers either. But, I did pretty well for my first time, didn't I?"

Xavier looked down into her beautiful violet eyes and felt such love and pride swell inside himself. She truly was a gift. "Aye, little one. You did very well."

He lowered his head and brushed his lips against hers in a tender kiss that had her melting against him. She wrapped her arms around his waist, holding on as he took the kiss deeper.

"Enough of that," Galan said playfully, pulling her out of his brother's arms. "I will be taking our mate for a walk while the rest of you set up camp. Come, mate. Let us go explore a bit."

The three other males grumbled as they shot him the evil eye, but Galan simply winked at Alexis, making her laugh. He took her hand in his as he led her away from the group. "I am very proud of you, sweetling. You have taken to being a Dragon Warrior's mate as if you were born for it."

She smiled as she bumped her hip against him. "I thought you said I was…born for it I mean."

He lifted their joint hands to press a kiss to her knuckles. "You were. In all the long years we have traveled the universe, we have longed to find the one female that would complete us. From the first moment we saw you we knew you were meant for us. Finding you has been a blessing."

"But how?" Alexis didn't mean to push the subject, but she really was interested in figuring out exactly how this mating worked. "How did you know I was the one for you?"

"We felt it the moment we arrived. Perhaps it is our magic that leads us to our perfect mate. One look at you was all it took, but it was more than that. I felt as if my very soul was reaching out to yours. Our race is one that feels deeply, far more than humans are capable of due to our ability to blood bond. It is a sacred thing, allowing someone else access to your mind, but it also allows those who are bonded a deeper relationship. We cannot hide anything from one another. There is no fear of deception or untruth between us, and you never have to doubt our feelings for you."

That was true.

Without the blood bond Alexis had felt as if she had been going crazy. Anger, jealousy and hurt had ruled her emotions, sending her careening into a dark place. She had feared losing them. The attraction between them had been there as soon as they arrived, but she had written it off as pure lust instead of understanding it was something more. She was used to betrayal, of people thinking that she was unworthy. With her mates everything was different. She had no doubt that she was their first priority now. It was going to take some time getting used to, but she wanted it, wanted the life she would have with them more than anything.

They walked through a break in the trees and came to the waterfall. To Alexis this had always been a magical place, and she was glad she could share it with them. The waterfall was set back into a large pool of crystal clear water that was where the area had gotten its name. Lava rocks heated the grotto area, making it lush with moss and ferns that hung down from the stones.

"This is beautiful, sweetling. Thank you for sharing it with us."

“This area is on the border of what we call the safe zone. South of this is mostly ocean and desert land that we call the badlands. The Alliance still hasn’t really expanded with major cities through those areas. There are outposts there, but rebels are still a problem.”

“And these rebels do not like living by Alliance regulations?”

“No, they don’t. But then again, the separation between the elites and other citizens makes it pretty hard to be equal.”

“Enough serious talk. I want to enjoy you while I have you all to myself,” Galan growled.

She laughed as Galan lifted her onto a large, flat rock, seating her in front of him. She automatically parted her legs, allowing him to move closer to her so his erection was pressing against her core. She felt a throbbing between her legs as her body reacted to his closeness. Stars, he felt so good against her that she wanted to feel their naked bodies pressed together. She wrapped her arms around his neck and tilted her head back, inviting his kiss.

Galan didn’t make her wait. He kissed her softly, brushing his lips back and forth over hers until she couldn’t stand waiting any longer. She opened her mouth and thrust her tongue into his, loving the deep growl that rumbled in his chest. She felt her nipples harden, aching for his touch. His expression was harsh, so serious as he gazed down at her when he pulled back. The intensity in his glowing silver eyes made her insides flutter.

Gathering her courage, she tapped into the magic inside her and will both of their clothing away. His eyes narrowed as his cock slapped against her bare mound. The power she had been gifted by them was amazing, and talk about easy access when she wanted it.

“You sway me from my purpose so easily, mate,” Galan growled.

“I would think your purpose would be the same as mine,” she teased as she wrapped her legs around him, trying to draw him closer. She looked down at the thick stalk of flesh throbbing against her. His enormous erection slapped against his rock-hard abs and she wanted to feel it moving inside of her. A pearly drop of liquid seeped from the tip of his cock and she reached down to swipe at it with a finger, bringing it up to her mouth. Her lashes fluttered at the sweet taste of him and she hummed in pleasure.

"Mmm…"

He tilted her head up so their gazes met again. Nostrils flaring, he looked like the warrior he was. She felt the strength of his need for her battering her system as if he was already inside of her. Confusion filtered in when he simply stared at her and she let her legs drop down.

Old habits of self-doubt seeped in as she studied him. "Is something wrong?"

"You are my dream, Alexis. On our world we would show everyone that you belonged to us by placing a mating torque around your neck. We do have one made, which we will give to you once we are back on our vessel, however there is something else we would like to do to bind you to us."

"All right," she said.

Galan smiled at her immediate agreement. Reaching up, he stroked a finger over the mark she wore on the right side of her face, right near her eye. He watched her flinch and anger surged through him at the thought of what the mark meant to her people.

"Don't be mad," she said, smiling at him. "The mark no longer matters."

"But it does. Close your eyes for a moment, sweetling."

Alexis closed her eyes and waited as she felt him press two fingers to the mark on her face. Her skin heated where he touched her and she could feel his magic flowing into her in a concentrated stream. When he stroked those loving fingers down her cheek she opened her eyes again. She didn't have to see it to know that the star tattoo that had labeled her as infertile was now gone. Galan had done that for her. He had erased her mark of shame because he knew how she felt about it. Tears of gratitude filled her eyes and he shook his head.

"Nay, sweetling. Do not weep."

"Thank you," she whispered tearfully.

"We knew the marking upset you. As our mate you will wear no mark but our own. As I said, we will place our mating torque around your neck to wear, however as Dragon Warriors we have our own mating ritual we would ask of you."

She nodded her head. "Okay, tell me what you need me to do."

"I know your aversion to the symbol you wore, but we would ask for you to allow us to mark you like us."

Her eyes widened. "Mark me…you mean like your tattoos?"

"Aye." Galan held his arms out, showing her the dark lines he wore proudly on his arms and torso. "When Xavier and I bound our lives to Thorn and Brydan we had our colors combined on our skin. The silver lines represent the House of Tesera and the gold represent the House of Volis. You are both now. Each of us will take a private moment with you to brand you with our magic if you agree. It is our way of sharing all we are with you."

"On Earth, elite soldiers mark their chosen woman with a tattoo next to her left eye when they claim her. The mark is a stylized design of their initials, but they themselves mark their left shoulders and arms as a sign to the world that they are bonded. I understand the meaning behind markings, and I want that with you. I want to belong to you. I would love to wear your mark, Galan," Alexis said softly. She took a deep breath as she prepared to lay her heart on the line. He deserved to know how she felt about him, and she wouldn't waste this opportunity to tell him. "Galan, I…I love you."

Out of all of her mates, Galan was the first to touch her heart. He was a warrior through and through, but there was something sweet about him. He was caring, and never hesitated to show her exactly how he felt about her. Through their bond she could sense that he had a sensitive heart, and his love for her was absolute and unending.

Galan's silver eyes burned like twin flames as he solemnly placed a fist over his heart. He laid his other hand over her heart while he stared into her eyes, forming a connection so it was impossible for her to look away. "You are my light, my love and my life. With this mark I share my magic and my heart with you. I vow to protect you, to ensure your happiness above all, and love you for all the days we are together in this life, until we are reunited in the next."

She felt the warmth of his touch heat up then she felt his magic flowing into her again. Looking down she saw a bright light shining from underneath his hand over her heart. Thin lines of silver swirled and flowed out from under his hand, up over her shoulder then down her back. She felt it moving over her right arm, trailing down to her hand so that her entire arm and upper torso was engulfed in his light.

When the light faded her right arm, shoulder and back were covered with a tattoo similar to his own. The design was beautiful. It looked like a silver dragon claw was cupping her right breast and it made her feel incredibly special to be able to wear his mark.

Tears were streaming down Alexis' face by the time he finished his vow. "I love you, Galan," she whispered.

"And I you, sweetling. You own my heart," Galan swore.

His mouth came down on hers, hot and hard. He gripped her hips, jerking her forward so she was sitting at the edge of the rock and she wound her long legs around him again. His hand slid down between them, stroking his fingers down her slit, spreading her juices over her lips of her sex.

She was soaking wet and ready for him.

"I need you, Alexis."

"Then take me. Mate with me, Galan."

Galan's lips claimed hers again as she guided his cock to her tight, wet pussy. His cock was rock-hard, and he felt ready to burst already, but he wouldn't come yet. Not until he was buried deep inside her. Fitting the bulbous head of his cock to her entrance, he slid forward, burying himself into her with one thrust. He froze, eyes going wide as her body accepted him with ease.

Alexis grinned up at him. "I think I'm getting the hang of this magic thing."

A chuckle rumbled in his chest. "Aye, you are. I was worried that I hurt you."

"I'm fine," she promised. "But you won't be if you don't start moving."

"Then I best get to it," Galan said then growled as he jerked his hips back, only to surge into her slick pussy again in a slow, steady thrust. He cupped her breasts with his large hands, pinching her nipples and he growled when her tight pussy clamped down on him.

Alexis drew his head back down to hers as they moved together. He was pumping into her slowly, driving her wild as he shoved his massive cock into her over and over again. He let out a low growl of pleasure as his lips moved down her neck. His fangs nipped at the soft flesh there, sending a shockwave of lust straight to her clit.

"Oh god," she moaned, letting him know exactly what he was doing to her. "It's so good. I love how your big cock feels inside of me. Faster, I need you harder."

"Slow, sweetling. I want to enjoy your muscles gripping me tight."

She could feel the strength of his control through their bond and she knew he was close to the breaking point. Squeezing her muscles on him, she tried to push him over the edge.

Galan let out a vicious growl as his hips bucked, thrusting into her with startling force. "Naughty, mate."

"Give it to me, Galan. Claim me hard and fast like we both need."

"You want me to claim you, mate?"

"Yes. Show me how much you want me, Galan. Do it. Fuck me and show me who I belong to."

"Mine," he snarled as his control snapped. "You belong to me!"

"Yes!" she cried out.

"Your pussy belongs to me. You are mine!" His voice was thick with lust as he pounded his hard length into her.

Alexis wrapped her arms around him, burying her face into his neck as his hands gripped her hips, pulling her to him as he stretched her tight hole with his cock. Their mutual pleasure collided inside of her through their bond, and she fed it back to him so that he was as crazy as she was. Shock filled her as she felt her teeth lengthen until she had fangs. An overwhelming urge pushed her, wanting the taste of his blood. Giving in, she sank her fangs into him, feeling their bond grow even stronger as she drank from him.

He snarled as he came, filling her pussy with his hot seed and his cock swelled, locking him inside of her. He moved his hand between them again, stroking her clit, so she bucked against him. Her cries of pleasure were muffled against his skin as waves of ecstasy slammed into her. She licked the wound on his neck closed then Galan gripped her hair and jerked her head to the side. He sank his fangs into her neck right below Xavier's mark on her and she let out a scream as another the brutal climax rocked her before the first one was finished.

"Wow, that was…wow."

"Aye, sweetling. Every time with you just gets better," Galan whispered tenderly as he stroked a hand through her pale locks.

She nuzzled against him, loving the scent of him surrounding her then froze as she remembered something that had her rearing back. She slapped his arm, shocking him even if it didn't hurt.

"What was that for?"

Her eyes narrowed. "Something else you forget to mention to me? I have fangs, Galan!"

"Ah…aye, you do." He shot her a sheepish smile as he stroked her cheek. "Forgive me for not mentioning it sooner."

She relaxed against him again, stroking her hand up and down the corded muscles of his back. "Somehow I have a feeling that there are going to be many more things that I'm going to find you guys forgot to mention."

"Time is up," Brydan announced cheerfully as he strolled out of the trees. His eyes sparkled with mirth as Galan let out a low curse. "I have been patient long enough. Since you are finished now, I intend on taking our mate on a ride."

"Is that a euphemism for more sex? Because you're going to have to give me a minute to recover if it is," Alexis said, making Brydan laugh.

Galan slowly pulled back, making her moan as she felt his cock leave her. He was still hard and she could feel his frustration at the interruption. She would have been embarrassed for anyone else to have come upon her and Galan while they were still locked together, but Brydan was also her mate so she was just going to have to get used to it.

She blinked as she looked down and suddenly found herself wearing a pair of tight leather pants and a thick gold-colored tunic. She looked up at Brydan as he held his hand out to her and allowed him to pull her to a standing position. She gasped as he produced a thick, fur-lined cloak out of thin air. He draped it around her shoulders, tying it at her neck as he winked at her.

"Where do you think to take her, Brydan? It is dangerous—"

"I will not let anything happen to her, have no fear, Galan." He looked down at her and the challenge was clear in his eyes. "Are you up for a little adventure, Lexie?"

"Of course I am!"

He stepped back from her, ignoring Galan's protests, and shifted into his dragon form. *"Climb on, mate. Let me take you flying."*

Alexis did a little happy dance then raised up on her toes to press a kiss to Galan's disapproving mouth. When he remained unaffected, she pouted. "I want to go flying with Brydan."

Galan sighed. "Then go, sweetling. Enjoy yourself."

She ran over to Brydan, using his wing to help boost her into position on top of his back. "Where are we going, Brydan?"

"It is a surprise."

"Take care of her, if not Xavier, Thorn and I will have your head," Galan warned.

Shock nearly had her falling off Brydan as he let out a plume of fire from his dragon nose. Galan didn't even flinch.

"Hold on, mate," Brydan said a second before he launched into the air.

Alexis let out a whoop of pure joy as they flew up into the sky. Brydan's large wings expanded, effortlessly propelling them over the land below. It was different then flying as a dragon herself. There had been a sense of power as she had cut through the sky as a dragon earlier. It was as if nothing could hurt her. But now, sitting on Brydan as he flew her toward the mountains there was an exhilarating feeling of being out of control, of being at the mercy of the elements. It didn't matter though because Alexis knew that Brydan would never let anything happen to her.

"Aye, mate. I would protect you with my life."

She smiled as she leaned down to wrap her hands around his large neck. It wasn't possible because he was so massive, so she simply laid down on his back and enjoyed the ride. Brydan took her high into the skies and finally landed on a mountaintop covered with thick snow. As soon as they touched down Alexis found herself in the arms of her mate.

Brydan pressed a sweet kiss to her lips and she smiled against him. “Did you enjoy yourself, Lexie?”

“Very much. I can’t believe how stunning it is from up here.” Alexis moved to the edge to look out over the beautiful mountain vista then turned back to him. “How did you find this place?”

“I went scouting while you were busy with Galan. Come, I have something to show you.” He took her hand and led her through a crack in the mountain, into the dark interior.

Heat blasted her like a slap to the face as Brydan lifted his hand and made her cloak disappear. She automatically adjusted her body temperature to the new terrain so she didn’t overheat. Talk about awesome. She could really get used to having magic.

Brydan led her through a dark tunnel, into a cavern filled with crystal stalactites and stalagmites that refracted the light filtering in from cracks in the ceiling. The room was filled with a kaleidoscope of rainbow colors, making it look like a fairyland from another planet. It amazed her that a place like this actually existed here on Earth.

“This is absolutely amazing!”

“I am glad you like it. I wanted to bring you somewhere beautiful,” Brydan said with a seriousness that surprised her. He was usually the most playful of the group and this sober intensity was new coming from him.

“Thank you.” She reached up to cup his face with her hands, drawing him down so she could kiss him. His arms wrapped around her waist, enfolding her into his embrace. The kiss was heated, filled with all the love and passion that they felt for one another. She wanted him. Wanted to feel his hands on her, to feel him inside her. She felt his steel-hard shaft rubbing against her stomach and it had a flood of wetness spilling from between her thighs.

It was shocking just how quickly the desire flared to life. She had just been with Galan, but now all she could think about was mating with Brydan again.

Alexis' hands moved down his chest and she pulled back, startled to find that he had removed their clothing while she had been lost in the kiss.

Laughing, she rubbed her body against his, causing his erection to swell further. "Someone is in a hurry."

She yelped as he picked her up, but she instantly relaxed in his arms and she continued kissing him. He carried her a few feet then lowered her onto what felt like a soft blanket he had placed on the floor, covering her body with his. Shifting, she tried to move so his massive body was cradled between her thighs, but he resisted. His large frame trembled as if the effort to deny her pained him.

"I love your breasts, mate. They are perfect," he purred as he cupped them. His head lowered and he sucked one of her nipples, making her shiver as it hardened from his attention. He moved onto the other one, nipping at it lightly. He pulled back and his glowing golden eyes seared into her straight to her soul. When she reached for him he shook his head, holding back.

His hand stroked her hair away from her face tenderly to soften his rejection. "There is nothing I want more than to spread you wide and take you like the beast that I am, but first there is much that I have to say and I vowed that I would before I took you again."

"All right."

He huffed out a breath and looked away. "I do not know where to begin…"

"Would this be easier for you if we had clothes on?"

"Nay. I need to feel you against me."

She also got the strong impression that he wanted her in a position where she couldn't run from him. Uncertainty poured through their bond and she stroked her hands over his golden skin, wanting to soothe him. Brydan was never hesitant. She wasn't worried about what he would say. Whatever it was wouldn't affect their relationship or how she felt about him. She loved him and knew that he loved her. "Tell me whatever it is you need to say. I won't run."

"I lost hope."

His whispered words were spoken so softly that she barely heard him, even with her enhanced hearing. Understanding that this confession was difficult for him, she waited, giving him the time he needed to say whatever it was that was weighing on his mind.

"A mate is not just a companion, Lexie. Mates are the other half to our souls and from birth finding a mate is the driving need for every male. As a Dragon Warrior it is even harder to be without a female to balance out the darkness that exists in the uncertainty of our lives. We travel, exploring different worlds, and even though I had Thorn and my blood brothers to keep my company, the long years were difficult for me."

He looked back down at her, their eyes meeting and she saw his were dull with sorrow. "I gave up hope of ever finding a true mate. For the last fifty years I faltered in my belief that we would find you, even when the others held their faith. I am two hundred years old, and that is a very long time to be without the other half of my soul," he said, almost as if it were a plea for her to understand.

She nodded slowly, stroking her hands over his shoulders. "It is."

"I took other females to my bed, more than the others. I tried to find someone that I could feel something for, but it never happened. I could never find a way to break through this barrier I seemed to have around my heart…until I saw you. I knew you were the one as soon as we arrived. I could smell the sweet scent of your skin, and I saw my future staring back at me through your beautiful eyes. It agonizes me to confess to you that I did not believe."

"Brydan…"

"I wanted to take you." The words burst out from him as though they pained him. "The very first thought I had was that I wanted to steal you. To transport you back to our vessel as soon as we saw you so no one could stop us from claiming you, even you. I did not care if it would have caused a war with Earth. I only thought of my own selfish need. It was dishonorable for me to even think it, but I had been prepared to do it. If the others had agreed, I would have taken you and given you no choice. Knowing this about myself is not something that sits well with me. It was dishonorable. You are my life, and I did not want to risk losing you."

Brydan felt the shame wash through him as he told her of his past mistakes. He knew in his heart that he didn't deserve her. Feeling the love and acceptance of all he was flowing from her through their bond humbled him and he vowed that he would never take the gift of her in his life for granted. Being with Alexis showed him why males of his kind wished for a mate from their birth. She was his joy, his heart, the other half to his soul.

"Brydan, you are my mate now. You don't have to worry about that. I forgive you, although I don't really think I need to. You didn't do anything wrong. I had a life before I met you too, and all that matters is that we are together now." She cupped his face with her hand and his eyes closed as he pressed against it.

His eyes opened again. "You undo me, Lexie. I love you, my mate, my heart. Now that you know my faults, will you consent to wear my mark?"

"I will. I love you and will never leave you, Brydan. I will wear you mark with pride."

Love for Brydan filled her. He was a warrior who felt that he had somehow failed her by giving up hope that he would find her through the long years, but she didn't blame him. Not at all. There was a gentle heart that he hid beneath his wicked sense of humor and his façade of not caring. The truth was he felt too much and he tried not to show it. It astounded her that he loved her so much that he would have risked war to have her.

How could she not love him in return?

Brydan's golden eyes were somber as he placed a fist over his heart. When he laid his other hand over her heart, she placed hers over his to strengthen their connection.

"Lexie, you are my light, my love and my life. With this mark I share my magic and my heart with you. I vow to protect you, to ensure your happiness above all, and love you for all the days we are together in this life, until we are reunited in the next."

She saw the light and felt the heat of his touch running through her body as she had when Galan had placed his mark on her, but she didn't look away from his eyes as she felt his magic seep into her. When the light faded, she lifted her arm and saw golden lines twined through the silver tattoo Galan had left on the right side of her body. She saw the dragon's claw tattooed on her right breast had dark gold threads woven through the silver. It was almost like she could feel Brydan and Galan touching her as she studied the design and she absolutely loved it.

"Thank you for loving me, Brydan. I don't blame you for losing hope. I am just glad we found each other. You weren't the only one who wasn't complete. I never felt like I fit in here, but with you, I've found my place. I love you, Brydan."

"You are my other half of my soul, Lexie. My heart is yours." Brydan swore.

"Show me. Make love to me and show me."

And he did.

With aching tenderness he kissed her. His touch showed her exactly how much she meant to him and she responded in kind, holding nothing back. When he moved over her, she welcomed him. And there in the cavern, surrounded by a brilliant array of colors, he made slow, passionate love to her until she was breathless and showed her just how much he loved her.

Chapter Nine

When Alexis and Brydan arrived back in the clearing, Thorn helped Alexis dismount from Brydan's back and took her hand to lead her back to the waterfall. On the way he couldn't wait to have her, and neither could she.

He held her in a passionate embrace as they came together in a clash of wills. Picking her up, he shoved her back against a tree and pounded himself into her until they both cried out in ecstasy. When the swelling of his cock dissipated, he swept her into his arms and carried her over to the pool fed by the waterfall.

She squealed with delight as he jumped in still holding her, immersing them both in the cool, clear water. They played together for a few minutes, splashing and laughing with one another until he settled them onto a cropping of underwater rocks close to the falls so the pressure of the water massaged their muscles. Resting her head on his shoulder, she sat in his lap, enjoying the peaceful beauty of the scenery and the warm sunlight shining down on them.

Alexis raised a hand to lightly stroke over the mark her fangs had left on his neck when she had bitten him and she felt him shiver at her touch. "Why do I feel this driving need to bite you when we're together?"

"It is the mating bond," Thorn replied, hugging her closer. "Every time we exchange blood it makes us closer. You want that with us just as much as we want it with you."

"That makes sense. I never was much of a biter...until now," she teased. "Although, I have to say the fangs came as a surprise."

He winced. "Aye, the fangs. I guess that is another thing I forgot to mention about the change."

Alexis chuckled. "Remind me to punish you later when I have the energy."

There was a long pause before Thorn spoke again and he tilted her face up so he could look down into her eyes. “Have we been pushing you too hard with our attentions, my love?”

“What? No! I love that you guys want me so much, and trust me when I say I am totally all for making love to all of you as much as we can.”

He stroked a gentle hand down her back. “You are so precious to us, my love. I know there is lots that you will still need to learn much about being a Dragon Warrior’s mate, but we have many years for you to learn everything.”

“I understand. Everything had been strange, but it’s all been so wonderful. I love being mated to all of you. What is going to happen now? I know you said that we could stay until I settle everything here, but then what are we going to do?”

“We will travel to whatever worlds you would like to see as we make our way back to our homeworld so you may see it. I want to show you the universe, to give you anything and everything you have ever wanted.”

“That sounds wonderful,” she said on a dreamy sigh.

“Since we are immortal, we have plenty of time to see whatever you wish.”

She jolted at that. “Immortal? Holy fucking shit storm! I know you guys were old, but shit, I didn’t really think about me being immortal now!”

His glowing golden eyes sparkled with mirth. “Something else we forgot to mention? Aye, we are immortal, although there are ways that we can be killed. Most Dragon Warriors that have lost their lives have done so in battle, so that is something you will never have to worry about. You will never put yourself in danger like that. I cannot bear to even think of losing you,” he growled.

“Don’t worry, Thorn. I have no intention of jumping into anything dangerous, unless any of you are in jeopardy that is.”

His eyes narrowed. “You will not—”

"I will not sit back and do nothing if one of you is in danger. I won't do anything that knowingly puts me at risk because I know all four of you would lose your minds, but I can't change who I am either, even for you. I am a soldier, and I need you to understand that."

Sighing, Thorn pulled her closer to him. "I think we need to just put you in a magical bubble where nothing can harm you. That is the only way I will stop worrying."

Alexis laughed softly as she absently reached down between them and stroked her hand over his semi-hard shaft and it quickly hardened as she touched him. "I wouldn't doubt you could really do it, too. You do like to catch me off guard."

Thorn let out a growl as his hips flexed forward. "You seem to like distracting me as well, mate. I cannot think of anything but being inside you while you stroke my cock like that."

Her hand stilled. She had been so focused on learning his body that she hadn't really realized that she had been stroking him. "I'm sorry, I didn't even—"

Thorn stopped her from pulling her hand away by wrapping his around her, keeping her fingers curled around his hard cock. "Do not stop. Feel free to touch me whenever you want, mate. We would love to have your hands on us at all times," Thorn offered in a strangled voice as she continued to torment him. "My body belongs to you, just as my heart and soul do."

She smiled shyly at him. "I've always been fascinated by male bodies, but I've never really felt comfortable with anyone before all of you to really explore how I wanted. I seem to be particularly mesmerized by your cock. It's so big and hard, and yet the skin is so soft. I love how it pulses in my hand. What are these?" she asked as she touched the three ridges underneath the head of his cock.

"It is the most sensitive part of our cocks and it rubs against the inside of your channel as we move inside of you." He purred as she rubbed her thumb against the ridges. "Your touch calms me and excites me all at once. It is amazing, the power you wield over me."

"You have only to look at me and I get wet for you. I've never felt this way before meeting you. I never knew I could love this way, but I do. I love you, Thorn. So much it scares me that it happened so fast." she whispered back, feeling his cock jerk in her palm at her words.

Thorn was her mate that she connected with on another level. He didn't hesitate to open himself to her, to provide whatever he could to ensure her happiness. His devotion was endless and absolute. She could feel the love he poured through their bond and it surrounding her like a cloak of warmth and happiness.

His golden eyes were practically feral as he stared back at her. "I will love you for eternity and beyond, Alexis. You are my every hope and dream. I need to be inside you, mate, but first I need to mark you, and then we can finish what you have begun."

Picking her up into his arms, Thorn carried her to the edge of the pool, sitting her on the bank so he was standing between her parted legs. He placed a fist over his heart then laid his other hand over her heart.

"You are my light, my love and my life. With this mark I share my magic and my heart with you. I vow to protect you, to ensure your happiness above all, and love you for all the days we are together in this life, until we are reunited in the next."

Thorn watched the light flow from beneath his palm to engulf her left side as his magic streamed through her system, marking her as his mate for all to see. He saw his golden tattoo covering the left side of her body, with his dragon's claw cupping her left breast right over her heart.

He was fiercely aroused looking at his mark on her and he felt pride surge through him knowing she belonged to him. No other male would touch her. He wouldn't allow it.

None of them would.

Looking down into her glowing violet eyes, he leaned down to take her lips with his in a brutal kiss. He opened his mind to hers fully, wanting to feel her inside him so they were one. He had no secrets from his mate, and wanted her to know him as completely as he knew himself. In return he wanted her to let him into her.

He wanted every part of her to belong to him.

Gently pushing her back so she was laying down before him, he spread her thighs so he could look down at her bare mound and a low growl of approval rumbled from deep in his chest. "You are so beautiful, mate. So pretty and pink. Look at all this juice spilling from your tiny little hole. I am just as fascinated by your body as you are with mine. You are mine. Mine to care for, to pleasure and love."

Alexis moaned low in the throat as Thorn's mouth lowered down to her and she jolted under him as his tongue swiped over her dripping slit. The taste of her exploded on his tongue, making him want more of her. He could feel her pleasure merge with his through their bond, and it heightened his own so his cock throbbed like an open wound.

"You are so sweet," he growled.

He fought down his own need and focused on bringing his mate pleasure as he held her body open for him to feast on. He lapped at the copious juices spilling from her pussy then concentrated on creating more as he shoved his tongue inside her hot hole.

"Thorn! Oh god, it's so good. Please…"

Her cries were music to his ears as she climaxed. The muscles of her cunt pulsed around his tongue as if trying to push him out, but he continued to shove back into her, drinking down her release.

He had never seen anything so stunning as his mate in the throes of her orgasm, and he wanted to see it over and over again. He wanted to drink down her juices until she begged him to stop.

He licked and sucked her tiny clit, shoving his finger deep inside her to drive her back to the brink of climax again.

"Come again, mate," Thorn demanded. "Come again and feed me your sweet release." He drove his finger inside her then added another, stroking in her while he sucked on her clit, making her cry out again. His other hand held onto her hip to hold her still as she thrashed beneath him.

"Mine!" He allowed the low, rough growl to rumble in his chest and was awarded as a new flood of liquid spilled onto his tongue.

"Thorn!"

She was glorious as she arched her back, and spread herself wide, offering herself to him completely. He licked and suckled her to another shattering release before he levered up over her and plunged his cock into her, unable to wait any longer. They rode out the waves of pleasure together, climbing higher and higher until his cock swelled and he gave himself over to the rapture of being one with his mate.

Alexis and Thorn walked back to their campsite holding hands and laughing as if they had been lovers for centuries instead of a matter of days. The sun had begun to set, but she smiled as they walked down a path that had been lit with torches that had obviously been left burning by her other mates so she wouldn't have to walk through the woods in the dark.

When they entered the clearing, she was shocked to see a large tent made of a shimmering bronze fabric was set up in the center. The tent reminded her of images she had seen in the archives of exotic desert tribes that lived long ago and she shot a questioning glance at Thorn.

"You did not think that we would make you sleep on the ground, did you? Remember, your magic males provide for you, always." Thorn gave her a gentle push forward. "Go to him. Xavier is waiting for you."

Giving him a kiss goodbye, she opened the flap and walked inside and came to a stop as she saw Xavier. He stood naked in the center of the room, right in front of the large wooden pole holding up the shimmering fabric of the tent. His perfect golden body bathed in the candlelight that filled the darkened interior of the tent. He had a warrior's stance, with his hands on his hip, legs braced apart and his long, thick cock jutting out proudly from between his legs.

Giving the room a once over, she was impressed at their ability to weave magic where there had been nothing but barren land. Inside the tent there was a huge mattress on the floor, with a dark-ruby colored blanket and various jewel-toned pillows on it, and off to the two sides of the room were two other comfortable looking pallets. They had explained to her earlier that each night she would sleep surrounded by two of her mates at her sides, while the other two slept separately. They would alternate nights, which suited her just fine, unless they pissed her off. Then she would banish all of them from her bedroom until she forgave them.

"Come here, Alexis," Xavier demanded. "Come claim what is yours."

His commanding tone didn't irk her. She could feel his joy at seeing her through their bond, and decided to embrace his playful mood by getting into character. Since he very much looked like a conquering warrior, she removed the shirt and pants Thorn had dressed her in after their time at the pool using her magic, and donned an outfit more fitting for a harem. The wispy material of the small top covered her breasts and she had created a skirt that sat low on her hips made of two small panels of cloth that barely hid the sight of her pussy and ass from view. She'd chosen a silver material that matched her lover's eyes, and knew she had surprised him with her daring.

Feeling bold, she stepped further into the light, walking toward him slowly so he could look his fill. She was pleased with the lust she saw shining from Xavier's bright silver eyes, and put a little more sway into her hips as she moved.

"Are you mine, warrior?" she whispered seductively when she was a few feet away from him.

"Aye, I am, mate. Body, heart and soul I am yours and pledge myself to you."

His dark vow thrilled her. Walking closer until she was right in front of him, she looked into his glowing eyes and reveled in the hunger she saw there. She knew that this day had been a testament of his self-control and his need to provide her with what she needed. Throughout the day she could feel him in her mind and knew that it had taken every ounce of his self-control not to seek her out and take her liked he wanted. Instead, he had allowed her time with her other mates to show her that her needs came first.

She knew how much that self-restraint had cost him, and it made her love him even more.

"If that is true, perhaps it is you who needs to claim me," she said coyly.

His eyes burned brighter at the challenge. "I claimed you the first time I touched you, mate. You will never doubt it again once I am through with you this night."

Being with her mates gave her a sexual freedom she had never known before. She could be herself, and she knew they would never make her feel silly or stupid. It was acceptance on such a level that gave her the confidence to do anything. They loved her for who she was and didn't want to change her. For someone who had never belonged before it was the most precious gift they could have ever given her.

"Then I will have to show you that you are claimed as well, my warrior."

Fire burned in her belly and she saw no reason to wait for what she wanted and she gave into her need to have him. He reached for her, but she avoided his grasp as she went down to her knees in front of him. Looking up at him, she saw the pleasure burning in his gaze as his jaw clenched.

"Claim me, Alexis. Open that pretty little mouth for me and suckle my cock, mate."

Alexis admired the massive erection bobbing before her and she gripped it, loving the feeling of him throbbing in her hand. She opened her mouth and her tongue came out to lick at the drop of pre-cum on the head of his cock, teasing him. She heard him let out a vicious growl and she enjoyed the way the thick stalk jerked in her grasp.

She did it again, looking up at him under veiled lashes. "I think my mate likes that."

"Aye. You know I do, mate. Now cease teasing me and suckle my cock. Show me who it belongs to."

His commanding tone had her thighs clenching to prevent the liquid heat spilling from her pussy from dripping down her thighs even as challenge had her snapping, "This cock belongs to me," she growled at him.

"Prove it," he shot back.

Alexis opened wide, taking him into her mouth as her lips wrapped around his cock. Using her tongue, she lashed at the three ridges underneath the head of his cock, relishing the harsh snarl that tore from his throat. She could feel his pleasure surging through their bond, and her hand went down between her own legs to stroke at her clit while she sucked him.

"Nay, mate. That is my pussy. This night you do not get to touch my pussy without my permission. In fact, I believe with four mates you will never have any need to touch it yourself."

Her eyes narrowed at his command and she removed the hand from between her legs and reached up to grab his ass instead. She felt the taut muscles clench in response and she drew him in until the head of his massive cock hit the back of her throat then pulled back only to do it again. Her grip tightened possessively on the base of his cock and she started working her mouth over him, showing him she owned him.

Alexis felt his hand shove into her hair, but he didn't force her to take more of him. Instead he anchored himself as she pleasured him, and the sharp pain as his grip tightened made her even hotter. She let out a moan as she began moving her head faster, sucking and stroking his cock.

"Fuck, it feels too good. No more, little one. I do not want to spill my seed down your throat this time. Enough."

Pulling at her hair, his hips moved back so his cock left her mouth with a pop. Frowning in disappointment, Alexis wanted to protest but when he reached down and threw her onto the large bed she smiled in anticipation. Spreading her legs, she removed her clothing with a thought, allowing him to see her slick pussy waiting for him.

"Look at how wet you are, little one. And it is all for me. Tell me. Tell me who you belong to." Xavier growled.

Wanting him too much to deny him, she whispered, "You."

"Louder. Say it louder," he demanded harshly as he knelt down between her legs.

"I belong to you, Xavier," she yelled at him as she jerked at his hair. "Now you show me."

He reached between them, and purred as his clever fingers moved through the slickness seeping from her pussy. "I think this is proof, mate."

"Not enough," she panted, wanting to impale herself on his fingers that stroked and teased her slit.

"Then spread your legs wider and invite me inside you, mate. Do it now!" he commanded and she quickly did as he asked. Before she could say anything more, he levered over her and shoved his cock deep inside her pussy, thrusting until he filled her completely. She gasped as her body strained to accept him, but the slight burn had her pussy creaming even more as his rough possession.

"Oh god, Xavier!"

"Do you like that, mate? Do you like the feeling of my cock filling your tight little pussy?"

"Yes," she moaned, wanting him to move, to stroke inside her, but he held still.

"You belong to me. Your pussy and your pleasure belongs to me." He stroked her face lovingly, startling her with the gesture. "And who do I belong to, mate?" he asked softly.

"Me," she whispered, knowing it was true. "You belong to me. Mark me, Xavier. I want you to mark me as yours."

The approval she saw in his glowing eyes filled her heart with joy. He rolled them to the side then placed a fist over his heart and laid his other hand over her heart.

"You are my light, my love and my life. With this mark I share my magic and my heart with you. I vow to protect you, to ensure your happiness above all, and love you for all the days we are together in this life, until we are reunited in the next."

The light flow from beneath his palm to engulf her left side as his magic marked her as his mate for all to see, completing the tattoo so that both sides of her body had the gold and silver lines etched on her. She felt their possession, their mark on her like a phantom touch that teased and tantalized even as it comforted her. It made her feel like she was being embraced by all four of them. When he ran his fingertips lightly over the dragon's claw covering her left breast it was a stroke that went deeper than her skin, straight to her core.

"I love you, Xavier."

"I love you, too, Alexis. I have something else I need to ask of you."

The hesitation she sensed within him had her sobering. His silver eyes glowed with intensity as he pushed her onto her back and braced himself over her, his cock throbbing inside her pussy so they were intimately connected. "I want to plant my seed inside you."

She smiled saucily at him. "I want that, too."

He shook his head slowly and she watched as his throat worked when he swallowed. Stars, watching his throat shouldn't turn her on, but it did. His serious expression had her sobering and after a long pause, she began to worry.

"Is something wrong, Xavier?"

"Nay, mate. It is just…I want to put my babe in your belly. Now."

Shock filled her. "What?"

"Using my magic I can try to ensure you conceive when I cum inside you this eve." He paused for a moment. "The others thought to give you time to accept your new life, but I cannot stop thinking about seeing you swell with our babe. Is it too soon for you?"

She blinked up at him. "Is that even possible?"

"I have never done so before, but if you are willing I would like to try with you."

Tears prickled her eyes. Xavier was her passionate warrior and she knew no matter his rough exterior, he had a tender heart that longed for love and acceptance as much as she did. He touched a part of her that she'd never let anyone else see before she met him.

During all the long years he had stayed strong for the others. As their leader, he had never spoken of his desire for a family out loud, but it had always been there. The ache in his heart had only grown stronger as they waited to find their mate...as he waited for her. His love for her made her feel like she could accomplish anything, and the fact that he was offering her a dream touched her soul.

"I love you, Xavier," she whispered softly to him as she pulled his head down to touch his lips with hers. "I would love to have your baby. Let's do it. Let's make a family together."

"I will love you forever and beyond, mate" he vowed, his voice shaking with the conviction of his words. "All that I am is yours."

He shifted, sliding his cock out of her then pushed forward again seating his cock to the hilt inside her. His eyes never left hers as he began to make love to her so sweetly it had the tears spilling out of her eyes.

He made a sound of protest as he leaned down to lick at the salty drops. "Do not weep, mate."

"I love you, Xavier. I love you so much. I didn't know I could feel such love."

"And I for you, little one."

He took her lips in a kiss that sealed their lips together, stealing her breath. His tongue plunged into her mouth as his strokes sped up, the fire burning inside of them too strong to hold back. She moaned into his mouth as he began stroking inside her, stretching her around the thick stalk of his cock as he fucked her.

Alexis felt her climax building and her arms wrapped around his neck, keeping their lips locked together as their tongues danced together. She whispered words of love through their bond, feeling their bond strengthen as he poured his own emotions back to her. The intimacy of speaking to him in her mind only added to their connection. Her legs began to shake with the intensity of the upcoming storm and she locked her ankles together at the small of his back as he plunge into her faster, making the bed shake with every thrust. His glowing silver eyes captured hers, making it impossible to look away.

"I'm going to come, Xavier."

"Do it," he growled. *"Come, mate. Give it to me."*

Overcome with the feeling of him moving inside her, she let the pleasure take her and came so hard her body burst and stars exploded behind her eyes. *"Xavier!"*

The world around her spun out of control, her body bucking beneath him and her hands gripped his sweat-soaked skin, needing something to anchor her as he rammed into her, over and over again. Her pussy clamped down on his cock so hard he could barely move inside of her as her muscles pulsed around him.

He was relentless as he prolonged her climax by nailing the sweet spot high inside her so that the pleasure continued to sweep through her until it bordered on pain. He continued to draw it out, thrusting heavily as he forced his massive cock in and out of her tight hole making her moan.

He continued to pummel her, his large body braced over her, his thighs holding her wide as he brought her closer to another shattering release before she had even recovered from the first. He impaled her with fierce determination holding her hip in a punishing grip as he drove into her desperate lunges.

"Too much...it's too good!"

"Never!" he snarled. *"It is never too much. Come again, Alexis. Come on my cock and take me with you, mate. Let me fill you with my seed and give you my babe."*

Alexis let out a scream as her release struck her with the force of a meteor. She felt her fangs growing and the need to bite him became overwhelming. With him deeply entrenched in her mind, he tilted his head for her, giving her access to what she wanted. She savaged his throat with hot, wet kisses before sinking her teeth into his neck, shivering as the taste of him burst onto her tongue.

Xavier let out a low snarl as he jerked her head to the side. Finding his own mark on her neck, he bit down, sealing them together in the moment of perfect passion. Raw ecstasy swept away his control and his cock swelled inside her. Hard, heated jets of his seed shot straight into her womb and his let his magic flow freely as he emptied himself inside her.

Light engulfed their bodies, surrounding them with pure love. She felt each heated pulse of his semen fill her, and when the spark of life settled inside her, she knew. A sob of joy slipped from her lips and Xavier let out a load roar worthy of a war cry. A huge grin spread across his handsome face and she smiled back at him through her tears.

They had done it.

Not only had she mated with all four of her mates today, making their bond even stronger than it was before, they had created a new life together.

Her greatest wish had finally come true.

Chapter Ten

The atmosphere around the camp was festive when Xavier and Alexis finally got the energy to get up and join the others. Each of her mates took turns kissing her senseless as they all celebrated the news that she was pregnant with their child.

They enjoyed a large meal as they sat around a large campfire. She was amused by their desire to feed her, but she couldn't argue with the way they pampered her. They fed her until she felt like she was going to burst, rubbed her feet and did whatever they could to make her feel special and cared for. Long into the night they share stories of their lives when they were young so that they could get used to the idea of having a baby of their own.

All four of her males growled in anger when she told them about her childhood and the process she had undergone when she had turned ten. They vowed that nothing like that would ever happen to a child of theirs. She had a sinking feeling that any children they had together would be spoiled rotten, but it warmed her heart when she saw the joy in all their faces as they spoke of all the things they wanted to pass down to the next generation.

She wasn't too comfortable when they began talking about teaching their children how to fight with swords and learning how to be warriors. When she asked them what they would do if they had a girl, all four of them froze in fear. They swore that their daughter would never be allowed to mate with a male because none would ever been good enough for her. It would have been funny if they hadn't been completely serious.

At one point, she jerked in shock when Brydan said he wanted at least ten children. "Yeah, we can do that…when you guys learn how to give birth."

Brydan had winced at that. "With our magic—"

"It's still probably gonna hurt like a bitch, so let's just see how this first one goes before you have me giving birth to an entire unit myself."

He had placed a soft kiss on her lips as he agreed and she couldn't be annoyed with any of them when it was so obvious they were thrilled with the idea of starting a family.

Later that night as she lay safely tucked between Galan and Brydan, she thought back on all the changes that had happened in the last few days. It was amazing that she had known them for such a short time, but with all of them constantly in one another's minds, it was like she had known them for years instead of days.

Every hour she was getting better at navigating her way through her mates' thoughts and memories, learning all she could about them and their lives before she met them. They held nothing back from her, keeping their minds opened completely so she was able to see inside their hearts and souls with no hesitation.

She knew all four of them worried that they were asking too much of her since she would be leaving her home for them, but she was looking forward to their future together. She loved her job, but it wasn't enough to hold her back from heading out on a new adventure with them. She loved her mates enough that she would go wherever they wanted with no reservations. She would miss her friends, however Galan had assured her they had the capabilities for her to stay in contact with whoever she wanted.

"What is wrong, sweetling?" Galan asked. She was draped over him and he reached down to remove her hand from her idle exploration of his cock to lay her palm over his heart so she could feel it beating. She did seem to have a hard time keeping her hands off their cocks whenever they were naked together and all of her males loved having her hands on them, even if it were just a comforting touch not meant to arouse.

"Nothing. I'm just thinking about everything that has happened these last few days."

"Overwhelmed?" Brydan asked as he curled into her from behind. His hand moved over her to cup her breast, tweaking her nipple gently.

"Not really. I'm more amazed that I have accepted all of these exciting new changes without blinking an eye."

"You were meant for us, Alexis," Galan said softly. "You have accepted everything because this is where you were always meant to be…our mate."

"Rest now, mate, our babe needs his sleep and so does his mother," Brydan said gruffly as he nestled his cock between the globes of her ass.

"You mean *she* need her sleep," Alexis teased, making both Galan and Brydan groan.

"Nay, not female. We will have to kill all the males that look at her if we have a female child."

"I am going to have nightmares now," Galan growled.

Feeling better now, Alexis closed her eyes and drifted off to a peaceful sleep.

The next few days went by like a dream.

The days were filled with laughter and fun as she spent time with all four of her mates, separately and together. At night she fell asleep cuddled between two of her males, so she slept safe and protected.

On the day before they were set to leave their quiet getaway, Xavier and Thorn quickly jumped out of the pool where all of them had been playing and took up a fighting stance, a silent snarl on their faces. With their enhanced hearing they could hear a sound coming from behind the trees on the far end of the clearing. Brydan pulled her out of the water, keeping her behind his large body as

Galan dressed her in black leather pants and a matching vest just like they wore.

Cursing herself, Alexis realized for the first time since they had left the guest suite that she didn't have her blaster with her. It didn't matter though. All four of her mates had conjured up wickedly sharp swords that gleamed dangerously in the sunlight. She knew any rebel that was stupid enough to challenge them were in for a rude awakening.

Lust curled in her belly as she took them in. They were warriors, strong and true. It was a new side of them that she had only seen in memories, and the reality of it was…extremely arousing.

Thorn shot her a glance and raised a brow. "Really?"

"Perhaps we will have to explore this…appreciation you have for us later, mate," Galan whispered into her ear, causing her to shudder.

"You can count on it," she replied.

"Come out and show yourself," Xavier called out and growled furiously when no one moved out into the open. His entire demeanor had changed, altering to that of a true warrior, a protector of what was his and Alexis knew that no harm would come to her while in their care.

"They might not understand you," Alexis said to all of them through their bond. *"If these are rebels who have never gotten a language implant, they won't be able to understand your language. Let me try."*

She could feel their immediate rejection of the idea and she rolled her eyes at their protectiveness. Making sure her voice carried, she yelled out, "Come out. We know you're there. Show yourselves. You don't want to make us chase you."

"If they are rebels you are to stay back," Thorn warned her. "Remember your promise. Do not put yourself in danger."

She sent warmth and assurance to all of them through their bond, telling them that she wouldn't do anything foolish. "It's not like you couldn't just poof them out of existence with your magic if you wanted too."

"We try not to use our magic that way. There is always a cost to using magic, and it takes lots of energy to take a life. Plus, it is just lazy and we do love a good battle," Brydan said with a wink.

To their surprise what came out from behind the trees wasn't rebels set on attacking them, but two small, terrified, dark-haired teens stepped out into the open.

"Put your swords away," Alexis hissed at them, trying to step around Galan to move forward. He held her in place and she growled at him. "They are children. Can't you see how scared they are?"

Galan sighed as he released her but followed closely as she walked forward. "Hello, there!"

"I have scanned the area and they are alone," Brydan announced, letting his sword fall so it was pointed towards the ground. *"I will continue to monitor the area."*

"Who are you?" the boy asked, his voice shaking with fear. The boy was around thirteen or fourteen and Alexis could see that the little girl hiding behind him was a few years younger. Both of the youths were dressed in rags that told her they were from poor, probably from a rebel family that lived on the outside of Alliance law.

"Don't worry. We won't hurt you," Alexis said softly as she drew closer to them. She saw that the boy held a small, knife in a hand that shook with fright.

"Don't come any closer! My sister and I didn't do anything wrong. Just let us leave…we won't bother you," the boy called out while the little girl peeked around her brother's back, holding a crude fishing pole clutched in her hands.

Thorn sighed. *"We do not usually like to use our magic on non-hostiles without their consent, but if we do they will be able to understand us."*

She knew that he was asking her permission for him to do it. It spoke of his honor and integrity, and she loved that he wanted to make sure she wouldn't be angry if he manipulated the children. "Go ahead, love."

Thorn and Brydan held out their hands and a few seconds later Thorn spoke to the children. "We will not harm you. You have nothing to fear from us."

Galan, Thorn and Brydan made the children gasp in amazement as they made their swords disappear into thin air. Xavier chose to keep his and slide it into his belt at his side so it was out of the way but still accessible in case anyone had followed the children into the woods.

"You may join us if you wish," Galan offered. With a natural ease that impressed her, Galan took her hand and sat down on a bench close to their campfire, pulling her onto his lap as he did.

Obviously intrigued, the kids took a few steps closer. Their eyes wide, they shuffled closer, but made a wide gap around where Xavier stood watching them with his arms folded.

"What are you doing?" Alexis admonished. *"You're scaring them. Stop it."*

Xavier heaved out a sigh and moved to sit down next to her on the bench. *"We do not know why they are here."*

"Why don't you try asking them instead of staring at them like they're criminals?" Alexis muttered then she smiled at the children. "Hi, my name is Alexis. These are my mates, Galan, Xavier, Thorn and Brydan."

The little girl looked at her with wide eyes. "You have four mates? Is that like a bonding unit?"

"Yes, it is. I am very lucky to have four wonderful males in my bonding unit."

"I don't want a bonding unit," the little girl said, moving closer to her brother who put a comforting arm around her. Alexis could see the scroll tattoo on the right side of the girl's face and her heart ached for her as she felt waves of pain and fear coming from the young girl.

"My name is Simon and this is my sister Marissa. Would you really have chased us?"

"Aye we would have," Brydan said cheerfully. "And we would have caught you too." He flicked out his hand and lit the campfire using his magic, delighting the kids with his display.

"Wow! How did you do that?"

"We are magic," Galan said with a wink.

"You aren't Alliance then?" Simon asked.

"Nay, we are Dragon Warriors from another world, but our mate Alexis used to be with the Alliance."

Simon and Marissa exchanged a look filled with fear before they both schooled their expressions. Alexis instantly wanted to soothe them. "I am no longer with the Alliance," Alexis said carefully. "I am now a Dragon Warrior too. If you are worried you are going to be in trouble for poaching on Alliance land, don't worry."

Simon relaxed at her words. "We know it's wrong, but our father said we had to come here and find enough fish to sell at the market…or else. He is too busy drinking with his friends to come himself. Plus, if we get in trouble he said we have a better chance of getting away."

Anger surged through her and she felt the answering call from all her mates.

"Their father needs to be beaten," Xavier growled.

Fascinated, Simon sat down on the bench studying Xavier, more at ease with them after seeing the anger on their behalf. The young girl seemed enthralled with Brydan.

"You have pretty hair."

"Why thank you, little angel," Brydan said with an amused gleam in his glowing eyes.

"Why aren't you in the Alliance anymore? Are you a rebel now?" Simon asked Alexis.

She shook her head. "No, I'm not a rebel. I stopped being a part of the Alliance when I mated with my Dragon Warriors."

"I wanted to join the Alliance, but my father wouldn't let me. I tested well and was slated to be an elite. My father got into some trouble and we had to move before I left for the Academy." Simon said. "Plus, I can't leave my sister. Our father intends to sell her when she turns eighteen. I'm going to get us away from our village, but I will have to make sure I can take care of Marissa before we escape. I won't leave her behind."

"Nor should you," Xavier growled. "We can make it so your father will allow you to leave. We would be pleased to fight him for you."

The two teens gaped at them. "You would really do that?"

"Aye," Thorn said with a nod. "We would."

"I don't want him dead..." Marissa said softly. "I just don't want to live with him or allow him to choose my fate for me."

Alexis thought for a moment. "I can still get you into the elite program if you still want to join the Alliance. Your DNA is already on record so it will be just a matter of registering you."

"I can't leave Marissa and I'm fourteen now. It will be harder for me to get into the program."

"That won't be a problem. You could bring Marissa with you. There are places in the city where she would be taken care of. Scrolls are treated very well, I promise. I'll speak with Commander Spartan and—"

Simon's eyes grew wide. "You know Commander Spartan at high-command?"

Alexis smiled. "Yes, I do. Very well in fact. He's a friend and well as my former commander. I can contact him now if this is something you would like to do."

"Are you for real?" Simon asked after a long moment of simply staring at her.

"She does not say what she does not mean." Brydan said as he stood. "Make your call, mate. Now come, younglings. I bet neither of you have ever ridden a dragon before."

Alexis laughed as Brydan and Xavier led the children off into the open area and shifted into their dragon forms. Xavier created harnesses for Simon and Marissa to sit on the dragon's backs and they took off into the skies.

Galan held Alexis on his lap while Thorn went into the tent to retrieve her wrist unit and they both sat with her while she made the call into Jax. When her commander answered the call his eyes nearly popped out of his head.

"What the fuck is up with your eyes?"

Damn, she'd forgotten to block the video.

"Ah…well, it's part of being mated to my Dragon Warriors." She sighed. "Jax, I'm no longer human."

"Sorry, could you repeat that? I don't think I heard you right."

"You did. They converted me when we mated."

"I have no idea what the hell to say to that."

Quickly changing the subject, she filled Jax in about the kids that they met and was instantly relieved when Jax told her to bring them into the Capital.

"I'll handle it," Jax promised. "We will make sure both of them are taken care of."

"Thank you, Jax."

Gray eyes studied her through the screen. "Anything else you want to tell me, Lex?"

She shifted on Galan's lap and curiously found comfort in feeling his steel-hard erection beneath her. It was a reminder that she wasn't giving up her life. She was simply moving on to bigger and better things.

Much bigger…

"Commander, I ah…I would like to formally give notice that I will be resigning my position as a liaison officer."

Jax's lip quirked up at the corner. "I figured that, but I was waiting for you to say the word. I started the process already and you can sign off when you get back. I'm away from the Capital today. I'll have Archer come meet you. He'll get the kids settled and will help the boy enlist."

"Thanks, Jax."

Jax studied her for a long moment with his piecing gray eyes. "We're gonna miss you, Lex."

She felt her eyes prickling with tears. "I'm going to miss you too, Jax. I'll see you at the party tomorrow night."

"Count on it."

When the call ended, Alexis rested her head on Galan's shoulder and Thorn ran his hand though her hair. "I can hear the affection in your voice when you speak to him," Galan said. "Although I am not very happy about that, I am sorry you will miss your friends."

She wrapped her arms around him and held on, turning her head to place a kiss on Thorn's hand. "I will miss them," she admitted. "But as long as I have you, the rest doesn't matter."

"We will make you happy, love," Thorn swore.

She smiled. "You already do."

Chapter Eleven

"We do not have to go in," Xavier said gruffly.

Alexis took a deep breath to calm her nerves and squeezed his hand with hers. She knew that her own anxiety was driving her mates crazy, making them even more protective as they walked into the Hall of Regents where the celebration for the Dragon Warriors was being held.

Down the long corridor she could see that the usually stark, dark gray interior of the building had been decorated with streams of red material and banners highlighting the red and black symbol of the United Federation Command Alliance. Chandeliers had been brought in, filling the hall with light, and the sounds of laughter and merriment could be heard from outside the building.

Alexis hovered by the entrance as she saw that the hall was packed with people. Regents, along with high command elites and their families stood around talking and laughing while others perused the tables laden with food and drinks. It was a relaxed atmosphere, but in the Capital political posturing was always at play. Most of the regents were good men and women, but some of them were so focused on the rules that they didn't see how their decisions actually affected people in practice.

She didn't socialize much, and she was nervous about being the center of attention tonight. Aware that her appearance with the guests of honor was going to cause a stir, she had a duty to her mates and to herself to make sure she didn't do anything to shame them. She was dressed in a shimmering violet dress that Galan had created for her because it matched her glowing eyes her mates loved so much. The gown flowed over her curves like liquid amethyst, and the single strapped design reminded her of something an ancient goddess would have worn.

She was pleased when she had looked at herself in the mirror, but when she had stepped out of her room and saw the look on her mates' faces she had felt like the most beautiful woman in the universe. She knew everyone would see the mating marks covering her body and her mates were pleased that everyone would know she belonged to them.

Her warriors all wore black leather pants and black shirts with gold and silver dragon designs on the back that wrapped around to the front. They had changed each of the dragons' eyes to a startling violet color and it warmed her heart that they had done so in her honor. They would have stood out in a crowd no matter what they wore. They looked so handsome it took her breath away and heated her blood. They were less formally dressed than the elite soldiers and officers in attendance who wore their dress uniforms, but nothing could detract from their warriors presence or the fact that they commanded attention simply by breathing.

And they were all hers.

Alexis and her mates had cut their sojourn at the waterfall short, choosing to fly Simon and Marissa back to the Capital to make sure they were taken care of. She had been amazed how well her four mates had interacted with the children. It had brought tears to her eyes to see a glimpse into the future at how it would be when their own child was born and it was clear she had made the right decision to start a family with them, no matter how quickly everything had happened.

Galan has kissed her softly, and she knew he had been reading her emotions from the gentle way he caressed her back. "We will be good fathers, mate."

"You will be the best fathers," she had agreed, knowing it was true.

To everyone's amusement, Simon had seemed to gravitate towards Xavier, despite his gruff demeanor. After they had gotten back from their ride on the dragons Xavier and Brydan had created wooden swords and spent part of the afternoon teaching young Simon how to sword fight while Thorn and Galan had entertained Marissa and Alexis by creating the most beautiful flowers they had ever seen.

It struck her how different her mates were regardless of how similar they were in appearance. Galan was her sensitive lover. She knew he would teach their children kindness and compassion, while Brydan, her troublemaker, would teach them fun and how to laugh. Thorn was the serious one of the group, but there was an innate thoughtfulness to him that was enhanced by how observant he was. And Xavier…he was her gentle warrior. He had a quick temper, but his heart was full and generous.

Separately, they were a force to be reckoned with, but together they were unstoppable.

They had shared a meal together then they had flown back to the Capital, landing on the roof of the guest quarters. Xavier had sworn to her that he would make sure she was clothed properly when they landed since she was nervous about seeing the soldiers they had been going to meet. True to his word, when she had shifted back into her human form she was dressed in her pants and vest, just like the rest of her mates.

As soon as they had landed, she saw Commander Sullivan Archer grinning at her as he stood watching them with his hands on his hips. The wind teased his dark blonde hair into a haphazard style and his light brown eyes sparkled with laughter as he had approached them.

"That was bloody brilliant! And holy stars, Jax wasn't kidding. Your eyes are…well, shit, Lex. You look amazing!"

All four of her mates had growled at Archer, making Simon and Marissa giggle. Alexis had rolled her eyes at the male posturing, knowing full well that her mates knew she thought of Sullivan Archer like an older brother. Archer had introduced himself to the youths and arranged for two of his most trusted soldiers to take them to their new homes. Both Simon and Marissa were excited to go through the enhancement process, and they were grateful for the new lives they would have from now on.

Archer had pretty much invited himself to dinner with them and he had apologized to the Dragon Warriors, telling them that he was so used to treating Alexis like his little sister that he'd forgotten that her mates wouldn't appreciate how familiar he was with her. Once they relaxed a little, Archer got along great with her new mates. Especially with Brydan since they seemed to have a similar sense of humor.

Now, she wished that she had agreed to let Jax and Archer escort them since nerves had her heart racing and her belly tied in knots. It was their first public appearance as a bonded unit, and her introduction as a Dragon Warrior to everyone in the Alliance. This was an important night, and she didn't want to fuck anything up.

Pull yourself together, Donovan.

That gave her pause. Well, hell…

What in all the worlds was her last name now?

"Stop worrying," Xavier ordered softly through their bond. *"We would like for you to call yourself Alexis Volis Tesera."*

She relaxed and smiled up at him. "I think that is the perfect name. Okay, I am done stalling. Let's go in and find me something to eat. I have to keep my strength up if I'm going to satisfy my mates later…"

Xavier leaned down for a kiss, but they were interrupted when a voice called out.

"Alexis."

She froze at the sound of that voice, wishing she never had to hear it again. Painful memories swept through her mind. She felt her mates stiffen and their bodies braced as they went on alert, obviously feeling what she was. She turned her head and saw Draven and Cristof striding toward them from behind. Looking at them now, she couldn't believe she had once thought them the handsomest of men. They were nothing compared to Xavier, Thorn, Galan and Brydan, and the pain of Draven and Cristof's betrayal faded under the soothing balm of her mates' love.

Both men wore confident, cocky smiles on their faces that faded as they saw her glowing eyes. "What in the hell have you done to yourself?" Cristof exclaimed.

"We need to talk to you. Now," Draven ordered arrogantly, and she could feel his anger that she had eluded them for so long.

They were angry?

That was laughable consider what she knew was coming…

Alexis felt the instant recognition hit her mates, and the sounds of their furious growls were enough to scare the hardest of trained warriors. Moving faster than she could see, Xavier grabbed Draven by the throat, jerking him up off his feet while her sweet, normally gentle mate, Galan, shoved Cristof face-first into one of the columns lining the entrance so hard pieces of pulverized stone rained down on the floor at the impact. Fortunately, they had moved so they were slightly in the shadows so no one saw the confrontation.

She knew her mates were angry, but her jaw still dropped as she watched all four of her mates lose their minds in spectacular fashion.

"Never speak to our mate again," Thorn growled at Draven as Xavier simply snarled silently at the terrified man dangling from his grip. Draven wasn't a small man, but Xavier's casual display of strength made it seem like he was almost weightless. Draven gripped at Xavier's arms, trying to break free. Xavier simply ignored the feeble attempts to fight him off and left him dangling in the air.

"Forget you know her," Galan snarled at Cristof. "She belongs to us now."

"Who the hell are you?" Cristof gasped.

“We are her mates, and we protect what belongs to us. You have been warned,” Brydan said dangerously soft as his hand changed into claws and he gently tapped one sharp talon against Cristof’s cheek. “If you even look at her again, we will end you. Nod if you understand.”

Both Draven and Cristof nodded frantically, and she could see both men were turning a very interesting shade of purple from lack of oxygen.

“Let them go,” she said quietly. “They aren’t worth this.”

The Dragon Warriors hesitated then Xavier and Galan released them, letting the two men crash to the floor as they gasped for breath. Draven and Cristof stumbled to their feet then ran away as fast as they could, never once looking back.

“That was a little excessive, wasn’t it?” Alexis asked, hands on her hips, not really angry but more amused at how they had chosen to handle the men who had hurt her in the past.

Thorn wrapped his arms around her, drawing her close. “Nay, that was fun. They cannot hurt you any longer, but I believe we let them off too easily. I have the desire to hunt them down and beat them until they weep for mercy.”

“They don’t matter anymore,” she assured him, rubbing his arms affectionately. “What I felt for them isn’t even a fraction of what I feel for you. I love you, all of you so much.”

“And we love you.” Brydan paused as he shot her an amused glance. “You were really attracted to them? They were weak and I am surprised they did not soil themselves with the fear I smelled emanating from them.”

She choked on a laugh. “Well, you are an intimidating lot, and my taste in men has gotten a lot better.”

“Aye, it has.”

Unwilling to waste one more second thinking about her exes, Alexis let her mates take her into the party. They entered the hall as a unit with Xavier and Thorn at her sides, Galan behind and Brydan in the front so they were a united front. She could see that they had the attention of everyone in the room as soon as they walked out into the open area.

Strange as it was, the brief scuffle with Draven and Cristof had calmed her nerves. Secure in her place at the center of her new family, she held her head up high and put a smile on her face. She nodded in greeting at several guests and saw their shock as they noticed her glowing violet eyes and that she was holding hands with two of the Dragon Warriors.

"I think my new eyes might be a showstopper tonight," she teased.

"Your eyes are the most beautiful sight I have ever seen," Galan whispered back.

She was amused as both Thorn and Xavier growled as they caught a man eying her in appreciation. The man's eyes widened and he fled, taking off through the crowd. She laughed at the satisfied look on Thorn's face then had to roll her eyes when Xavier growled at another man.

"Behave yourself," she scolded.

"But you love it when I misbehave," Xavier growled back, playfully.

"I do. Let's just get through this evening without any more drama, shall we? Then we can go home and misbehave together," she purred.

"I think that dress is too tight. I do not like how these other males are looking at you," Thorn grumbled, looking down at her through narrowed eyes as they made their way through the crowd.

That made her laugh. *"They aren't looking at me, silly. They are looking at my very handsome, very large mates."*

"Nonsense," Galan scoffed. *"You are gorgeous, mate, and it gives me a thrill to know these males covet you but they cannot touch you...or we would kill them."*

"Aye," Xavier growled. *"We would."*

"And we would have fun doing it," Brydan said as he turned around to wink at her.

"You guys are so crazy," she said with a laugh. *"Just remember that I have magic now, so you need to be careful about who you flirt with tonight or I might have to get mean."*

"We do not flirt," Xavier protested, insult in every word.

She shot him what she hoped was a haughty expression. *"See that you don't or I might have to put these new claws to good use."*

Galan let out a purr as he stepped forward so he was pressed against her back. *"I love when you get all possessive of us, mate."*

She felt his cock thicken against her back and couldn't help rubbing her ass against him. *"I keep what belongs to me. Now, let's go have some fun."*

"There she is! Take her into custody!"

The voice rang out, startling Alexis as several soldiers moved forward to surround them. The crowd of spectators gasped as they moved back, giving them a wide berth. Xavier, Thorn, Brydan and Galan let out vicious growls as they moved to protect her, leaving her no doubt that the man who had spoken was talking about her.

What the hell was going on?

"Touch her and I will rip your arms off and beat you with them while I watch you bleed to death," Xavier snarled.

"Really? That's just disgusting…" Alexis said, too shocked for a proper response.

"I think the description was quite accurate," Brydan said then snarled viciously at the soldiers closest to him. That had the officers stopping instantly and looking at each other warily as they refused to come any closer.

"They will not touch you, mate," Thorn swore.

"I know," she said, sending her mates a wave of assurance. The last thing she wanted was a brawl in front of all the guests.

Regent Harold Dexter, an older man who wore his arrogance like a cloak, strode up to confront them. “Officer Donovan, you are under arrest.”

Xavier, Thorn, Galan and Brydan all growled at his announcement, and Alexis knew that the older man had no clue how close he was to death by the haughty look on his face.

“If you think we will let you take our mate you are insane,” Thorn said with a mocking laugh.

“Your mate?” A woman asked as she walked up. Alexis turned and was relieved to see Regent Marie Wyland join the group. She was known to be a fair regent and an impartial voice during conflict. Her jaw dropped in shock as she finally noticed Alexis’ glowing eyes, and it was obvious that this farce was all Regent Dexter’s doing and the other council members didn’t know anything about him trying to have her arrested.

“Aye, our mate,” Galan replied harshly. “You will never take her from us!”

“She has violated—”

Regent Wyland cut Regent Dexter off before he could finish speaking. “I think we need to finish this discussion somewhere in private. This isn’t the time nor the place for this, Harold.”

Alexis laid a gentle hand on Xavier and Galan’s arms and felt them shaking with the need to defend her. *“We need to talk to them.”*

“Nay, not if they threaten you we do not,” Galan said.

“Please. I’m not scared. I know you would never let anything happen to me.”

Xavier was enraged and it took all his willpower not to lash out at the stupid fuck who dared to threaten his mate. Never before had the urge to kill taken him so strongly that he would have attacked the man in the middle of the party without a second of regret. If not for his mate, he would have torn the man to pieces and let his brothers take care of the soldiers surrounding them, but he couldn’t because he knew that would upset their mate even more. Still, despite the calm she tried to portray, the distress emanating from her was enough to make him feel feral.

That small human male had embarrassed their mate, and that infuriated him. It shouldn't be allowed. No one should ever make his beautiful, little mate feel anything less than the priceless gem she was. He calmed a little as he felt Alexis' faith in them and her absolute belief that they wouldn't let anything happen to her. Focusing on that, he conceded.

Xavier sighed then turned his furious glowing eyes on Regent Wyland. "We will speak with you, but call off your guards first," he said sharply. "We will not have anyone threatening our mate or will we react in kind. This is the only warning you will receive."

Alexis was relieved when Regent Wyland barked out an order to the soldiers to stand down while Regent Dexter sputtered furiously. They were shown into a room the regents used as a hearing room for disputes. She was obviously on trial so Alexis thought it was fitting. She held her head up high, showing no fear under the circumstances and felt her mates approval.

Xavier, Thorn, Galan and Brydan surrounded her protectively, all of them looking at the people who entered the room through narrowed, furious eyes. She could feel the anger pouring from her mates and was holding onto her own by a very thin thread. It was wrong. This whole entire situation was totally fucked up, but she didn't want to cause a rift between the Dragon Warriors and humans that could jeopardize future relations between the races.

So, she would see this through.

Several regents positioned themselves in a half circle, automatically taking a position of power, but that didn't bother Alexis. She knew who was the greatest threat in the room, and it wasn't the humans. With their magic, there was very little the regents could do to them, but Alexis was walking a tightrope to keep her mates from attacking anyone who insulted her. She could smell the fear coming off of a few of the regents and smiled in response.

Good. They should fear them.

Regent Wyland started off as she stepped forward and shot a hard look at the man who has created the drama. “Regent Dexter. Would you care to explain why you chose to make a spectacle during this celebration?”

“Officer Donovan is a disgrace as a liaison officer and should be held accountable for her actions and abuse of her position,” Regent Dexter spewed out as he waved a hand in the air. “We cannot have officers disregarding the rules and regulations so flagrantly without punishment.”

Alexis bristled at the irate tone of the regent charging her. Her only crime had been falling in love with her mates, and there were no rules in place about that. She could feel that her mates sensed that she needed to handle this herself for her own piece of mind. Feeling their pride in her swell, she took a step forward to address the panel of regents.

“You speak of rules and regulations when all I did was follow my heart. Yes, I understand that there are guidelines in place for liaison officers not to overstep their positions, but there is no rule regarding a choice to bond with any visitors on a permanent level. These males are my mates and I have chosen to bond my life with theirs.”

“You stupid girl, that wasn’t your decision to make,” Regent Dexter sneered.

“Insult my mate again and I will rip out your throat,” Xavier snarled softly as his hands changed to lethal looking claws. He took a step toward Regent Dexter, making the other man pale.

“If not mine than whose?” Alexis shot back as she placed a calming hand on Xavier’s arm. She could feel the muscles straining beneath her palm and knew it was taking every ounce of his control to stop from launching himself at the spiteful man. *“Please calm yourself, my love. They can't do anything to hurt me. I know you will protect me, but there is no need."*

"I do not like that fucker," Xavier growled.

"Nor do I," Alexis said and gave a little laugh to calm him. *"But I really don't want to get banished from Earth, so let's play nice with the others. Trust me, I got this."*

"We will trust you, mate," Brydan interjected. *"But if that poor excuse for a male makes another attempt to take you from us, I will transport him straight into the middle of a large boulder."*

She shot a startled look at him. *"Can you really do that?"*

Brydan shot her a look and she saw that his glowing eyes were sparkling with veiled amusement. *"I do not know, but I am willing to try."*

"Officer Donovan," Regent Marks said gently, jumping into the fray. "We can't have officers doing something like this without addressing the council—"

"Why not?" Regent Spartan said as he folded his arms and frowned fiercely at the others. Alexis felt gratitude sweep through her as Jax Spartan's father spoke up on her behalf. "If they wanted to mate with her and she with them, why the hell would she have to speak to us about it?"

"This could impact all humans—" Regent Marks began.

"But that is the point…Alexis is no longer human," Commander Sullivan Archer said as he entered the room followed by Commander Jax Spartan. Alexis could see that her two friends were furious and she was pleased when they came to stand with her and her mates, showing everyone exactly who they supported.

Gasps sounded from a few of the regents and Jax nodded his head, crossing his arms over his chest. "And she is no longer Officer Donovan either. She had already informed me of the situation and had been cleared of duty, which is how Regent Dexter knew about her mating the Dragon Warriors."

"After the fact. She resigned after the damage was already done," Regent Dexter argued.

"So what?" Jax fired back. "You think she should have resigned before she mated to them? What kind of fucked up logic is that?"

"Careful Commander, you are on thin ice," Regent Dexter warned.

Jax scoffed at that. "You want to come at me, Dexter? Bring it. You might want to remember you aren't above the law either. Challenge me at your own risk."

"What do they mean that you are no longer human, Alexis?" Regent Wyland asked.

"Just look at her eyes and those markings covering her arms and back," Regent Spartan said. "It's obvious she is different and I have to say it looks good on her."

Alexis felt her mates love flood into her through their bond, giving her the courage to say what she had been holding back for so long. It was time for the regents to truly understand what had happened and why she had made her decision to mate with them. This was her opportunity to speak up for all the women who didn't have a voice, and she was determined not to waste it.

"When I agreed to mate with my Dragon Warriors they converted me." She ignored the shocked murmurs and continued. "I believe it was fated that I meet Xavier, Thorn, Galan and Brydan. The only reason you are hearing about any of this now is because I am permanently bonded with my mates and not hiding it. And you forget, Regent Dexter, I am an empath, and my gifts have only been enhanced by my conversion. Back in the hall I could sense your daughter Marianna's satisfaction when you confronted me. You seemed fine with her flirting with them earlier this week at the dinner the regents hosted, and I have to wonder if that has anything to do with your actions tonight."

“How dare you!” Regent Dexter roared. “I have no idea what you are talking about.”

“It is true,” Thorn growled. “I heard you speaking to your mate about how your status would be increased if we were connected to your family, but we had no interest in your daughter. We knew Alexis was meant to be ours as soon as we met her.”

“I have also heard Regent Dexter’s opinion on infertile women before, and it gives me extreme pleasure to have this opportunity to tell you that you are a disgrace as a regent for calling us wastes of resources,” Alexis announced. The room erupted with furious exclamations and her mates growled in anger.

“You go too far,” Regent Dexter seethed.

“She does not!” Galan snarled. “I have seen the memory for myself.”

“Yes, I shared that memory with my mates.” Alexis agreed then addressed the rest of the room, ignoring the man who had once made her question her own worth. “We share a mind bond and they have seen the truth. I understand that there are reasons for the protocols in place for testing and placement of elites, and I even understand the marking to designate which woman can help further the human race, but some of your rules cause more problems than they solve. To some, the star marks us as unworthy, and to others it marks us as targets. As an infertile female I have been limited to the life I could have here on Earth. In fact, all women are limited on Earth to some degree and I am glad that I had the opportunity to choose my own bonding unit, unlike most fertile women.”

“You know there are reasons for our system,” Regent Marks rebuked.

“Yes, but that doesn’t make it fair. It is easy for you to say as a man who has no idea how women feel. On the Council of Regents there are no infertile females allowed on the panel so those women have absolutely no say unless you allow it. You speak of rules and regulation, but I have worked undercover to help find those officers that have abused their positions of power to blackmail and take advantage of infertile females and it happens more than any of you know."

"This is very troublesome," Regent Marks murmured.

"How do you think the infertile women feel?" Alexis asked, surprising all the regents with her vicious, inhuman growl. "Even the way you have chosen to confront me about this matter shows absolutely no respect for me or my mates whereas any bonded unit would have a private audience with you. Instead, Regent Dexter chose to do this at a celebration held in honor of my mates. The fact is he would be fine with his own daughter bonding with the Dragon Warriors, but since I was worthless because I was infertile I have committed a crime in his eyes."

"Damn their celebration," Brydan muttered. "They can take their honor and—"

"Brydan…" Alexis murmured his name.

"We deeply regret the timing of all of this, and for the reason," Regent Wyland said.

"Make no mistake, we agreed to speak to you as a courtesy because our mate wanted us to, but as Alexis is no longer human you have no hold over her," Galan added.

"Agreed." Regent Spartan said. The hard look in his eyes dared anyone to question him, and they didn't.

"Centuries ago our own world had rules in place that were made to counter our lack of females, but there came a time when those rules needed to be changed. Perhaps you should consider your own rules and who it is damaging," Thorn said. "Matters of the heart have no bearing in the political arena. Alexis was destined to be ours and there is nothing you can do to change that."

Alexis let her love flow to her mates through their bond and straightened to her full height. "I have been given a chance for something greater, to be better and a chance at real happiness. I found love and with my mates. I'd regret if this alters relations between Dragon Warriors and humans, but I won't let you come between me and my mates. We do not plan to stay on Earth long and will be leaving soon. Still, I would like to know we will be allowed to come back and visit."

"You will always be welcomed here, and I assure you the regents will be taking care of this matter internally," Regent Spartan assured, flicking an icy look of distain at Regent Dexter. "This matter is now closed."

"This is outrageous!" Regent Dexter screamed.

"Guards, why don't you escort Regent Dexter home where he will remain until we can investigate his actions properly."

The man shouted, making a fool of himself as two elite soldiers removed him from the room. A few of the other regents left now that the excitement was over until only Regents Spartan and Wyland were left.

"You've got a mouth on you, my boy," Regent Spartan said to his son.

Jax snorted. "Who the hell do you think I learned it from, old man? I told you that asshole was going to be a problem."

"He was voted into office."

"By other regents and high command. If you allowed the officers to vote he would have never gained his position," Alexis pointed out.

"This is true, and something we have to consider," Regent Wyland said with a nod.

Brydan frowned. "You are saying that the governing body will be the ones to decide if they want to limit their power by giving the vote to the people? Is that not what had gotten you into trouble already?"

"No system is perfect, unfortunately," Regent Spartan explained. "But it was made clear tonight that there is a need for some changes to be made. Hell, I wouldn't mind if someone else took my place on the council."

Jax laughed. "What, you retire? Mother would kill you if you and my other father were home with nothing to do but bug her."

"I can't imagine you giving up having a say what is going on," Archer added.

Regent Spartan sighed. "I'm afraid they are right." He turned his attention to Alexis and her mates. "I am very sorry this happened when tonight should have been a celebration of your mating. Please allow us to have you over for dinner to make up for it before you leave with your mates."

"Sir—" Alexis began, but she was cut off as Regent Spartan cupped her face in his hands. She felt the affection the older man felt for her and smiled up at him. When she was young, she had always wished her family had been as loving as Jax's parents were, but even the brief times she had stayed at their place during breaks from the Academy they had made her feel welcomed.

"Let us celebrate with you, Alexis."

"I would like that," Alexis said softly. The older man smiled and pressed a kiss to her forehead, making her mates growl in warning.

Regent Spartan chuckled. "You are going to have your hands full with these four, Alexis. Come, Jax, Sully. I want your take on what we should do about this business with Dexter. Marie." He gestured to Regent Wyland, Jax and Archer and the four of them left the room together.

"I am sorry that man ruined your party," Galan said as he pulled Alexis to him as soon as they were alone. He pressed his lips lightly against hers, needing the connection with her after having their mating challenged by strangers.

"It wasn't ruined," Alexis countered. "I'm actually glad I got to say a lot of that stuff. I would have never had the opportunity to speak in front of the Council of Regents like this otherwise."

"This system is flawed," Brydan grumbled as he pressed against her back.

"It is," she agreed, turning her head for his kiss.

"Come here, mate." Thorn said as he pulled her away from the others and took her lips in a long, heated kiss. When he pulled back, Xavier claimed her, lifting her off her feet as his mouth slammed down on hers.

"I did not like having them challenge our mating. No one can take you away from us. We vow to protect you always."

"I know you will, big guy." She smiled. "Now that the regents know that we are mated there is nothing to worry about. Why don't we go enjoy some of the decadent food they have provided then we can go home and continue our celebration in private?"

"That is a good idea," Galan agreed, his glowing silver eyes taking on a wicked gleam. "I say we reward our little mate for defending our mating by seeing just how many times we can make her orgasm this night."

Her knees went weak as arousal flooded her system and she couldn't help but grin.

That sounded like a damn good plan.

Epilogue

Thorn chased their mate down the long corridor of their space vessel, laughter rumbling in his chest as she turned to smile back at him as her pale hair streamed out behind her.

"You think you can escape me, mate?"

Her only response was more laughter as she kicked it in gear and ran faster.

Gods, he loved her.

It had been a month since they had left Earth, and it was almost like setting out for their first adventure exploring the stars as all four males saw it through Alexis' eyes. Thorn loved sharing all the new experiences with her. He wanted to lay worlds at her feet and shower her with all the riches they could find on the different planets they visited. She didn't need any of it though. Alexis said all she needed or wanted was her mates, and she showed them just how much she loved every moment they spent together.

Being on their vessel was different with Alexis on board. She brought a light to the cold interior that made her a joy to be around. Her vital presence chased away the memory of those long, lonely years they had spent exploring without their mate by their side, and she filled Thorn's heart with a love so strong he had a difficult time believing she truly belonged to them and wasn't just a figment of his dreams.

They had converted the master bedroom into her room, decorating it with items and colors of her choosing. They knew she preferred gold and silver because it reminded her of their eyes, but they had added accents of purple hues to the room in her honor. They had also made sure to add a large shower into the bathing room to go with the large pool they used to cleanse themselves.

Because they used the gel-like water from their homeworld, they didn't need any additional soaps or other products, but they had made sure to stock plenty of her favorites before they left her home planet.

At night two of them slept beside her, cuddled together on the large bed in the center of the room while the other two retreated to their own quarters or took turns monitoring their flight path. It was on those days that he slept alone that Thorn counted down the seconds until she was awake, waiting impatiently for the opportunity to see her again. He didn't like being away from her for very long, and he knew the others felt the same way.

She was their greatest treasure.

Love filled him as she cast another look back at him, and he slowed his steps, not wanting to put an end to their fun before she was ready. He loved the way her ass looked in the black warrior's pants she liked to wear, but she had paired it with a bright purple halter top that left her back bare so he could see their mark on her. She ran towards the control room where Xavier and Galan were plotting a new course that would take them to a space station they wanted to show her.

The doors slid open soundlessly and Xavier and Galan turned as she entered the room at a dead run. "What is this?" Xavier asked as he caught her when she jumped into his arms. She giggled as she pressed her lips to his, wrapping her arms around his neck.

"Save me!"

Thorn hurried into the room after her, smiling as she turned and shot him an impish grin.

"You think Xavier can protect you from me?"

"What has our naughty mate done now?"

She wiggled free of Xavier's arms and hurried over to sit on Galan's lap, curling into him as if for protection. "I haven't done anything."

"I think someone is lying," Galan growled as he nipped at her lower lip playfully.

The doors slid open again and Brydan stomped into the room. "I cannot believe you tripped me, mate! Remember that statue those females on Helix gave us?" he asked with a low growl.

Xavier's brow rose. "The one that they gave us because they thought we were gods?"

"Aye, that is the one," Thorn responded. "Someone just decided to release it into space from one of the ports."

"You threw away a gift given to us?" Xavier asked with a growl, but his glowing silver eyes sparkled with mirth.

"There was no need for you to keep a statue those females made that highlighted your cocks, thank you very much," Alexis huffed out.

"I believe someone is jealous," Galan murmured as he nuzzled her neck.

Brydan smirked down at her with his hands braced on his hips. "Aye, I would say she is."

Her eyes widened comically. "Ha! Like you are one to talk! You melted the hair combs gifted to me from those nice D'Airians!"

Galan choked on a laugh. "You melted her hair clips?"

Brydan's smile faded. "They should not have given you anything! We are your males and we provide for you!"

"Galan had already asked me not to wear them and I agreed. You didn't need to melt them into a pile of goo." She batted her eyelashes at him innocently. "It wasn't like it was a statue of me naked."

That had all four of her mates frowning fiercely at her. "It better not be. Ever. No other male sees you bare," Xavier said as his eyes burned bright with anger at the thought.

Galan growled when Alexis shifted on his lap, making his cock swell in his pants. Their sweet, little mate knew exactly how feral it made them to think about other males seeing her beautiful body. She belonged to them and they would kill anyone who touched her or tried to take her from them.

"Perhaps you need a reminder of who you belong to," Galan whispered. Reaching up, he cupped her breasts, and he smiled when he felt her nipples harden against his palms.

"As if I could forget…" She swayed toward him, letting her lips brush lightly against his. When he moved to take the kiss deeper, she pulled back.

Standing, she sent them each a look that had their blood pressure rising before she turned and headed for the door. "Well, I think it was a fitting punishment. Brydan destroyed a gift given to me, so I booted your statue out of the port."

"After you smashed it to pieces," Thorn added.

She wrinkled her nose at him. "Whatever. I'm going to our room. If you are done missing your statue, you may join me. If not, you can just stay here and sulk."

She barely made it across the room before she was swept up in Thorn's arms. He loved how she immediately wrapped her arms around his neck and seemed to melt into him. "We do not sulk. You may get rid of whatever you like if it angers you, my love."

She sighed as she rested her head on his shoulder. "I'm sorry, I just love you so much I can't stand it sometimes."

Tenderness filled Thorn's glowing eyes as he carried her down the corridor with the others quickly following. He stroked her hair and pressed a kiss to her temple. "You are entitled to feel jealous of our life before, but never doubt that you are now the only one in our hearts."

"I know that. I was just having fun, but Brydan goaded me into losing my temper."

"Something that I am extremely good at doing it seems," Brydan said with a wink as the door to the master bedroom slid open. He let out an exaggerated sigh. “But I shall miss that statue…”

“You’re lucky I just tossed it and didn’t smash you over the head with it!” She lunged out of Thorn’s arms, and Brydan caught her to him with a laugh, tumbling them down onto the large bed.

“I believe that pregnancy had made you volatile.”

She gripped his hair in her fist and gave him a yank forward. “You like getting me fired up,” she accused.

“Aye, I do.”

“Then make it burn, Brydan.” She crushed her mouth to his and she willed their clothes away so their naked flesh rubbed together causing a firestorm of heat to curl in her belly. They could always do this to her. All it took was one touch and she was instantly ready for them. Her body softening against their hardness, her pussy slickening as she craved their possession.

Brydan placed a hand over her stomach over the small bump, his eyes gentling as he studied her. “Are you feeling okay?”

The last few days she had begun to have morning sickness that debilitated her for hours as soon as she woke up. She already had her bout for the day, but every time she got sick, her mates hovered around her like crazy men. She had forced them to make a promise to her that they would go to a medical facility with other women when she was due to give birth. There was no way in hell she wanted to be stuck with them when she was ready to give birth. If they had such a hard time dealing with her when she was throwing up, she was not looking forward to giving birth with the four of them going to pieces around her.

"I’m fine. Don’t worry about me. Now, lie back and take your punishment," she whispered and he automatically maneuvered them so he was lying back on the bed with her straddling his thighs. His erection was throbbing with need and he stiffened when her hands slowly stroked over the tense muscles of his abdomen, down over his straining staff. His body jerked under her touch and he sighed with pleasure as he watched her.

Alexis lifted up a little and positioned his cock at the entrance of her pussy, pressing down slowly so she felt every inch of his thick erection sinking into her hot depths. Her head fell back on a moan and she felt Xavier's hard body pressing against her back, his cock sliding against the crease of her ass as his fangs nicked at her neck.

"Are you still missing your statue?" she asked, teasing him with her slow movements.

"Fuck the statute," Brydan growled as he gripped her hips. He groaned as she tightened around him. She was so hot, so wet that her juices were soaking them both as she welcomed him inside her body. The sweet scent of her arousal filled the room and it made him hungry for a taste even as he refused to leave the haven of her body. His hips surged up, pushing deeper inside her as she began moving over him.

Xavier rubbed his fingers over the tight rosebud of her ass, using his magic and her own slickness to push inside of her. He worked his fingers inside of her, stretching her as she squirmed beneath him. Her breathless cries ignited a wild hunger inside of him that made him desperate to have her.

He would never get enough.

Through their bond he felt the sharp pain of his entrance fade as he worked his fingers inside of her. He adjusted his touch according to what brought her the most pleasure and he watched his brother and their mate kissing as he moved into position. Pulling his fingers free of her grasping flesh, he pushed the head of his cock to her tiny entrance and began filling her ass with his cock.

Alexis pushed back slightly, taking more of him until the head of his cock popped past the tight ring of muscles. He stilled, allowing her to get used to him before he pushed forward. Being inside of her was like coming home. When her body relaxed he slid deeper, filling her completely as his pushed her down over Brydan and his large body covered her back.

"Easy, mate. Just relax and let us love you."

Looking at their marking on her skin, he slowly began rocking his hips. "You are amazing, Alexis. Your tight ass and sweet little pussy were made for us to fuck, to love."

He began pumping his hips against her faster, using longer strokes that countered Brydan's so they kept her at the edge of release.

"More, I need more," she cried out. "Please, I'm so close. Fuck me, Xavier. Fuck my ass while Brydan fills my pussy. Do it, claim me."

"You are so impatient, mate," Xavier growled, but gave her what she asked for. Gripping her hips hard, he began pumping into her fast and hard. His thick shaft rubbing against Brydan's through the thin barrier inside her and every stroke brought him closer to climax.

Brydan pulled her down and took her lips in a brutal kiss as the force of Xavier's thrusts pushed her onto his cock. "Let us give you what you need, mate. Let us love you."

"I love you," she sobbed as the pleasure seared her from the inside out. "I love you so much."

"As we love you," Xavier said as he pounded into her ass. "You are our everything. I love you, little one. I love you so fucking much I would die without you."

"Aye, you are our world, Lexie. I will love you until the end of time. Now come, mate. Come on my cock and milk my seed inside you."

"Aye, come for us, little one," Xavier demanded as he continued to pound into her ass with fast, hard thrusts. "Come and take us with you."

On their next thrust, Alexis screamed out as her body shattered and her body tightened, clamping down on their cocks like a vise.

Xavier pulled out of her, working his hand over his cock as he stroked himself to completion, spilling his pearly cum over her ass as Brydan exploded inside her pussy. His cock swelled, and another climax rocked her before the first had even ended. She slumped against Brydan, panting for breath and whimpered as she felt another hard cock rubbing against her ass.

"Shh, easy, mate," Galan growled softly.

A new fire burned inside of her as she was lifted up off Brydan and his cock slid from her pussy now that the swelling had gone down.

Galan laid her down on the bed, his large hands stroking over her soft skin, loving the feel of her. He parted her thighs and moved over her, sinking into her tight pussy to the hilt. Her muscles quivered and pulsed around him, taking a moment to adjust to the new intrusion then her body relaxed welcoming him into her depth.

"Every time it just gets better," he murmured as he began to move. "You feel so good, sweetling."

He began thrusting steadily, driving her wild as he sheathed himself inside her over and over again while Xavier and Brydan played with her nipples. He moved slowly, allowing for the intensity to build inside her until she was aching for more. She scratched her nails down Galan's back, knowing he loved that bite of pain and was rewarded as his hips surged against her. Wrapping her legs around his hips, she moaned as he began pounding into her, relishing in the waves of love coming from all four of her mates.

Thorn moved into position beside them, gripping his long, thick cock in his hand as he watched them. "Come here, mate. I want to feel your hot little mouth suckling me. I love how you worship my cock with your mouth."

Pulling back, Galan helped her flip over so she could take Thorn's cock into her mouth as Galan moved behind her, pushing into her pussy from behind. Her lips eagerly parted, taking Thorn's cock in as she moaned from the pleasure of feeling Galan sinking into her wet heat with slow, steady thrusts. Thorn held still, allowing her to take him in at her own pace. She licked and sucked at his hard shaft, paying special attention to the ridges below the head of his cock as she used her tongue to lash over the sensitive flesh.

Tilting her head back, Alexis watched the pleasure burning in Thorn's golden gaze as she concentrated on taking him further into her throat. She swallowed around his shaft, enjoying the animalistic growls rumbling from him as her own muscles tightened around him. Her hand stroked the base of his cock, coaxing his climax so he was at the brink of release as Galan pushed her closer to the edge.

"Oh!" She pulled off of Thorn's cock to gasp out loud as her body began to tighten again. "I'm going to come, Galan. Please…come with me. Fill me with your seed. Give it to me."

"Aye, mate. Take it then!" Galan snarled as he pounded into her with renewed force. She lowered her mouth back to Thorn's cock, desperate to have him come with her and sucked him hard, milking his shaft with her fist when she felt him swelling.

"Here it comes," Thorn growled. "Drink my seed down, mate. Take it all."

He snarled as his cock exploded and his sweet cum exploded from the tip of his cock, shooting down her throat. His hand moved over hers on his thick shaft, helping her to milk every spurt of his release into her mouth as his cock swelled. Alexis gulped his release down greedily, loving the taste of his cum.

She screamed out and Galan reached down between them, pinching her clit with two fingers as he exploded inside her, his cum shooting from his cock in hot hard jets as he swelled inside of her. Her body bucked and her screams were muffled by Thorn's cock as she rode out the pleasure tearing her apart. The walls of her pussy convulsed, leaving her at their mercy when she was catapulted into pure bliss.

She was barely aware of Thorn pulling his cock from her mouth and Galan lowering her down onto the bed, still lodged deep inside her. She panted for breath as aftershocks rocked her body, her pussy flexing around Galan's thick shaft from her climax. Thorn lay down in front of her, stroking her sweat-soaked hair from her face, looking into her eyes as his kissed her. Gentle hands stroked her skin, soothing her with comfort that only came from love.

And there was love.

Between the five of them there was enough love to last them several lifetimes.

"Beyond that," Thorn whispered. "I will love you for eternity."

"We will love you for eternity." Brydan corrected. "Thank you for being ours."

"You belong to us," Galan said softly. "Just as we belong to you."

"Forever, mate," Xavier said as he gripped her hand with his.

Forever, Alexis thought.

Forever seemed just long enough for her to love her mates.

THE END

ABOUT THE AUTHOR

Laurie Roma lives in Chicago and mainly writes contemporary, romantic suspense, and sci-fi romance. She has always loved immersing herself in a good book and now enjoys the pleasure of creating her own. She can usually be found tapping away on her keyboard, creating worlds for her characters while she listens to music. Of course her playlist depends on her mood...but then again, so does her writing.

An avid reader of the romance genre, nothing bothers her more than annoying characters. Seriously, who wants a happy ending for someone that pisses you off? She loves tough alpha-male heroes and strong heroines that have brains as well as beauty. Her novels are filled with both passionate romance and down and dirty lust-driven interludes, as she believes both are essential to a good love story. She loves to hear from her readers and can be reached at mailto:laurieromabooks@gmail.com.

For all titles by Laurie Roma, please visit
http://laurieroma.blogspot.com/

3013: THE SERIES
http://3013theseries.blogspot.com

The 3013 Series

3013: MATED by Laurie Roma
3013: RENEGADE by Susan Hayes
3013: CLAIMED by Laurie Roma
3013: STOWAWAY by Susan Hayes